Marika

Andrea Cheng

SCHOLASTIC INC.

New York Toronto London Auckland Sydney
Mexico City New Delhi Hong Kong Buenos Aires

Ez a Mom

No part of this publication may be reproduced in whole or in part, or stored in a retrieval system, or transmitted in any form or by any means, electronic, mechanical, photocopying, recording, or otherwise, without written permission of the publisher. For information regarding permission, write to Front Street Books, Inc., 862 Haywood Road, Asheville, NC 22806.

ISBN 0-439-55696-1

Published by Scholastic Inc., 557 Broadway, New York, NY 10012, by arrangement with Front Street Books, Inc. SCHOLASTIC and associated logos are trademarks and/or registered trademarks of Scholastic Inc.

12 11 10 9 8 7 6 5 4 3 2   4 5 6 7 8 9/0

Printed in the U.S.A.   40

First Scholastic printing, March 2004

A Note on Hungarian Names

Names of people are given in the Hungarian way: the personal (or "first") name comes after the family (or "last") name. For instance, Marika's name is Schnurmacher Maria; her father is Schnurmacher Pal.

"Neni" and "Bacsi," meaning roughly "Auntie" and "Uncle," appear with the personal name only and are placed after it. These terms indicate friendly respect rather than actual relatedness.

Many Hungarian names contain accents or diacritical marks. For readability, these have been omitted. In the case of the name "Mitzi," the spelling too has been changed (from the Hungarian "Mici"), to reflect the correct pronunciation.

CONTENTS

Forgery

December 1939

My father, Apa, and my uncle Lipot mixed the ink. First it was too black, Apa said. Old ink would never be so black.

"So add some water," Uncle Lipot said.

"Maria, go get some water," Apa ordered. He'd been calling me Maria a lot lately instead of Marika, my usual nickname.

I came back with a cup of water. Apa complained that it was too full. They added drops of water to the ink, arguing about exactly what color old ink would be. When they finally agreed, they made me practice on a scrap of paper over and over again. I wrote the names, occupations, and religion of my parents and grandparents. *Katolikus*, Catholic, was of course the most important.

"Write smaller, Marika," my uncle said. "Do you think clerks in those days wrote big like first-graders?"

I felt the blood rush to my face. It was 1939. I was twelve years old, and my uncle said I wrote like a six-year-old. I tried again to write my grandfather's name, *Schnurmacher Henrik*, and *Katolikus* in my smallest, best calligraphic handwriting.

"Maria, that's too small. The clerks did not have eyes as good as yours," my father reminded me. "A little bigger."

I practiced some more, not too big and not too small. Finally they gave me the real thing, five blank documents. They had already used coffee to darken the paper. Now it was my turn to fill in the blank lines. Uncle Lipot leaned over me as I dipped the pen into the ink.

"Give the child some room," my father said. "How do you expect her to write when you are breathing down her neck?"

Uncle Lipot backed up. I finished the first *Schnurmacher*.

"If only we didn't have such a long name this would be so much easier," Uncle Lipot said.

"Stop talking, she'll make a mistake," Apa said.

"I was only saying that a name like, say, Toth wouldn't be so bad."

"If our name were Toth we wouldn't be going through all this," Apa said, motioning with his hands to the world outside the window. Then they were quiet as they watched me fill in the blank marked *Vallas*, religion. *Katolikus*.

I stopped to take a breath and rest my hand.

"Very good, Marika, very good. A clerk in 1870 could not have done better," Uncle Lipot said.

"Of course it's good," Apa said. "You know Marika has the best handwriting in the class."

"Not a talent she acquired from her father," Uncle Lipot said.

"Nor from her uncle," Apa added.

I picked up the pen to get started again. There were four more forms to finish.

"Take a longer break," Uncle Lipot said. "There's no rush to finish all at once. Your hand must be tired." He massaged my fingers in his big warm hands.

I shook my head. My hand was not tired at all. Just my head felt tingly. Uncle Lipot was right. If our name were Toth or Voros or Kis we wouldn't have any of these problems. It was bad luck that we were Schnurmacher so everyone knew we were Jewish. Why couldn't we just change our name? One day I would go to school and instead of being Schnurmacher Maria I would be Toth Maria or Kis Maria. What difference would it make to anyone? Anyway, we celebrated Christmas and Easter. My brother and I went to Catholic mass and religion class like all the other kids. We'd been baptized, and there were papers to prove it. When I grew up, I would change my name, and *zsido*, Jew, would be gone forever. No need to forge anything.

Once Kis Zoltan, a boy in my class, took his bad report card home, and instead of showing it to his father for the required signature he wrote his father's name by himself. Soon his parents were called in, and poor Zoltan was expelled. When I told Apa the story he had no sympathy for Zoltan. Forgery was a crime, he said.

"Now, Maria, remember this is for your father, Schnurmacher Pal. Be careful. Make the *P* an old-fashioned one, you know," Uncle Lipot said.

"She knows," said Apa.

I knew.

Finally four of the forms were signed and blotted. The ink was just the right color. The word *zsido*, Jew, was permanently erased from every birth certificate. We would be safe, Apa said.

My father was always worried. Bad things were happening to Jews in Austria and Germany. One of my cousins in Vienna couldn't go to university because he was Jewish. His older brother lost his job. I even heard Apa tell Uncle Lipot that his friend's son was snatched off the street just because he was Jewish. But Vienna was in Austria, far away from Budapest.

There was one form left. Apa said we would keep it blank for now. You never knew when a blank one might come in handy. Apa laid all the documents in a row on the floor to dry. Uncle Lipot sat back in the armchair, and I saw that his face was drenched in sweat. When I looked at Apa there were tears in his eyes. He tried to say something about how wrong it was to forge, but Uncle Lipot cut him off.

"She knows," he said.

I nodded.

MAXI

July 1934

When I was six years old, we went on vacation to our summer house in Vac, a small town on the Danube about two hours from Budapest. I discovered when we came back to our duplex that our apartment had been made into two, a big one for my mother, my brother Andras, and me, and a smaller one for my father alone.

"Why?" I asked my nanny, Mitzi Neni.

"What's the matter? You still have your own room, which is more than most people," she said.

I stared at the wall in the hallway and tried to remember how it had looked before we went to Vac. "Next time I'm not going," I said, stamping my foot.

"Little ladies do not stamp their feet," Mitzi Neni said.

"I'm not a little lady," I said, and she spanked me on my behind. Then Andras came and took me into his room. He didn't usually let me in there because he was thirteen, and he said I ruined his models, but this time he let me sit next to him while he worked on making a car with his Erector set. He even let me tighten a few bolts with the tiny wrench. He told me not to worry about the wall, it was only a few pieces of wood with plaster over them. I eyed the wall suspiciously. It looked solid to me.

"Why can't we live with Apa?" I asked him.

"That's just how it is. We will live with Anya, but Apa will not be far away."

"Why can't we all be in one apartment?" I persisted.

"It wasn't working out," Andras said. That was all he would say. What wasn't working out, I wondered. I could see how Andras's model car wasn't working out, but our apartment was working out just fine.

Andras got frustrated with the car. I went into my room, lay down on my bed, and hugged my doll, Maxi. Maxi was actually not a doll at all. He was more like a floppy puppet. My uncle Lipot brought him back from Austria, and when I first opened the package, my aunt Ila criticized him for bringing me a rag puppet.

"Why didn't you get her a porcelain doll?" she asked him. "Why this ugly pile of rags?"

"A porcelain doll for my Marika?" He shook his head and smiled at me with the twinkle he always had in his eyes. "I saw this one and I just knew it was perfect."

"He is!" I shouted, hugging Maxi tightly and swinging him around. Maxi became my best friend. My aunt Ila bought me a porcelain doll the next week, and I thanked her politely, but the doll stayed in its box, gathering dust under my bed. Once in a while Mitzi Neni took her out to dust her off.

"Why don't you play with this lovely doll?" she asked me. "When I was a child, I would have been so happy to have such a doll."

I shrugged my shoulders. "I don't like her, that's why. And neither does Maxi."

"You shouldn't say things like that about a gift, you know," she said, placing the doll back in its box under the bed.

After she left, I mimicked her to Maxi. "You shouldn't say things like that," I said.

I couldn't find Maxi anywhere. That was unusual because I always played with him in my room. I looked under my bed and even under the mattress, but no Maxi. Mitzi Neni was in the kitchen gossiping with the cook.

"Where is Maxi?" I demanded.

"Don't interrupt," Mitzi Neni said, and kept right on talking.

I tried again. "Where is my Maxi?"

"Little girls who interrupt will have their mouths frozen," the cook said, without even looking at me. I glared at her and left the kitchen. I searched all over the house for Maxi. Finally Andras came home and found me sobbing under the piano.

"Marika, what are you doing under there?" he asked.

"Looking for Maxi," I said. "I've looked everywhere but he's really gone."

Andras thought for a minute, then left the room. I heard him rummaging around in the garbage. He brought Maxi back to me with a little bit of egg stuck to his hair. I washed it out in the sink as best I could. Then Andras went to find Mitzi Neni. I left the door of my room open so I could hear better.

"That rag doll leaks sawdust all over the bed," Mitzi Neni said.

"But did you ask Marika if you could throw him away?"

"Ask a six-year-old child who has a much nicer doll under the bed?" Mitzi Neni couldn't believe her ears.

"Well, he is back on the bed now," Andras said.

After my nose stopped running from so much crying, I told the story of Max and Moritz to Maxi in German. It was about two little naughty boys, Max and Moritz, who got into trouble. They were caught and then punished. At the end they had their eyes pecked out by chickens.

After we finished the story, I told Maxi, "Now remember, Maxi, you are Maxi and not Max. Nothing will ever happen to you. Chickens will not peck your eyes out, and Mitzi Neni will not put you into the garbage again. Now listen carefully, Maxi, and you will learn German just like me. You never know, learning another language never hurts. That's what Uncle Lipot says, and he's the one who rescued you from the awful store in Austria and brought you to me. You must have heard German in that store. Funny you never learned it. Well, you never learn things if you don't want to. Uncle Lipot says that too."

"Marika, why did you name him Maxi?" Uncle Lipot was standing in the doorway of my room.

"Because it's his name," I said.

"But you could have chosen something more...less... less Jewish, you know, like Laci or Zoltan, Zoli for short. Wouldn't that be a nice name, Zoli?"

My eyes narrowed. "Some Maxis aren't Jewish. Max and Moritz aren't Jewish, are they? Anyway, how would you like someone to come around and change your name?"

"Frankly, I'd love it," Uncle Lipot said. "I'd throw out our Schnurmacher in a minute if I could."

"You would? What's wrong with it?"

"Oh, Marika, Schnurmacher is not a good name to have for the same reason Maxi is not a good name to have. These are Jewish names. Why should we be stuck with names that make us stand out?"

"But, Uncle Lipot, Schnurmacher is just the German word for braid maker."

"Yes, and Klein is the German word for small, but have you ever met a Klein who is not Jewish?"

"I have never met a Klein."

Uncle Lipot sighed. "Marika, you are a smart girl, but there is a lot you still don't know. Let me tell you what I know about Schnurmacher. A long time ago there was a prince who wasn't as bad as the rest. Now, he didn't exactly love the Jews or welcome them, but he let a group of Jews stay within his estate if they would work quietly and not cause trouble. The Jews did various jobs for the prince and his court. One of them made the golden braids that decorated their uniforms. The prince called this one Schnurmacher, and he must have been your great-great-great-grandfather. So now we are stuck with a Jewish name." Uncle Lipot stood up. "I am just warning you that Maxi is a very Jewish name and you might be wise to pick something more Hungarian."

"Uncle Lipot, Maxi is the name he has."

Uncle Lipot sighed, patted the top of my head, and left my room.

I told Maxi not to worry, that his name was just fine. Everything I had heard about being Jewish or not Jewish was crazy anyway. When I talked, Apa told me not to use my hands because that was a Jewish thing to do. Uncle Lipot said I was lucky I had such a small nose; nobody would think I was Jewish. Really, we were no more Jewish than Mitzi Neni or the cook. We had a huge Christmas tree each year that was decorated with the most beautiful angels and stars. Apa said religion was just an old-fashioned idea that didn't do anyone any good in the modern world, so it made sense to be just like everyone else: Roman Catholic. I agreed.

As I fell asleep, I told Maxi again not to worry, that nothing like what happened to Max and Moritz would happen to him. "The only thing you need to watch out for is workmen," I told him. "Make sure they don't come while I'm not home and divide this room up with wood and plaster the way they did to our apartment. That's the only thing we need to worry about."

COLETTE

September 1934

Mitzi Neni was sent to work for another family. My mother, Anya, said that it was time for me to learn French from a French nanny, now that I had turned seven.

"I already speak German," I complained.

"But that is not enough," Apa said. "You never know. You may live in France someday, and then you will be happy that you know French."

"In France? Why would I go so far away?" I asked.

"Marika, you do not know where life will lead you." Apa was irritated. "It may not be your choice. I would guess that my Jewish ancestors did not choose to leave Galicia." What was Apa talking about? Where was Galicia? Apa went on. "Marika, many things can be taken away from you, but you can never lose what you have learned. Learning languages is of the utmost importance."

"Colette is coming tomorrow on the train from Paris," Anya said.

"Why didn't you ask me first?" Andras demanded. "I happened to like Mitzi Neni, did you ever think of that? Of course not. All you think about is learning this and studying that. None of my friends have to learn so many languages."

His head was bent down and his shoulders were hunched. Anya told him to stand up straight, but he hunched some more. She was bent over too, and for the first time I saw that they looked alike.

Andras left the room and I followed him into the hallway. He turned and said, "You always hated Mitzi Neni anyway."

"She didn't like Maxi," I said.

"Maxi, Maxi. Is that all you care about? Mitzi Neni was better than some old French nanny. *Parlez-vous français?*" he said in a falsetto voice.

"I never said they should send Mitzi Neni away," I said.

Andras kicked at the floor. "Well, I will have nothing to do with that French mademoiselle," he said. "That's for sure." He turned and disappeared into his room.

"Andras?" I called.

He came to the door. I wanted to ask him about lots of things, about why everyone was so gloomy all the time, about the wall in our apartment. I still didn't see why Andras and I couldn't stay with Apa. That would make a lot more sense. Apa made the real decisions in our family. Anya only ordered the maids around, decided the dinner menu, and called the dressmaker to alter our clothes. Sometimes she played the piano for hours. When her fingers hit the wrong notes, she didn't notice. Anya was completely deaf in her left ear and mostly deaf in her right from scarlet fever. If we talked loud and she watched our lips, she usually knew what we were saying.

I imagined having breakfast with Apa every morning, hot cocoa and toast, just the two of us. But what about Andras? Maybe he could stay with Anya and I could go with Apa. That way it would be fair, two and two.

"What do you want?" Andras asked, irritated.

"Nothing," I said.

Andras put on his jacket, opened the door of the apartment, and left. I looked out the window and watched him cross the street and disappear down the hill. Where was he going? He didn't have friends close by. I hugged Maxi. It was my fault that Anya fired Mitzi Neni. Andras already knew French. The new nanny was coming just for me.

Colette was short and plump with big crooked teeth. When she spoke Hungarian with a French accent, I couldn't stop myself from laughing. Her face got red and she slapped my cheek.

I was so surprised at first that I just sat there. I'd been spanked plenty of times by Mitzi Neni, but they were more like taps on the behind. I ran to my hiding spot under the piano. Colette ignored me and dusted the living room.

After about an hour, she said, "Lunch is ready, Maria. Come to the table."

I lay on my back and counted the strings of the piano. The little hammers were pretty with their felt-covered heads. Colette kept looking nervously at her watch. My mother would be coming home from her shopping trip any minute, and if she found my lunch untouched and me under the piano, she would not be pleased.

Colette tried being stern. "Maria, this is no way to behave. Come out this instant."

I didn't answer.

She softened. "Come see Colette, *mon chou,* and Colette will fix your hair in two little ponytails like all the little French girls have."

Did she think that I wanted to look like some sort of French poodle? I stayed put. She tried ignoring me again. A few minutes later she came back with a bag of foil-wrapped chocolates.

"I'll give you one of these chocolate bonbons if you come out," she said sweetly. We got chocolate only on special occasions, and it was my favorite food in the whole world.

"How do I know you really will?" I challenged.

The outside door unlatched.

"I promise," she said, rolling a bonbon to me. I grabbed it quickly. My mother was taking off her coat in the front hallway. The silk lining rustled. The door to the living room began to open. I crawled out from under the piano. My legs were so cramped from crouching all morning that I almost fell. Colette tossed the whole bag of bonbons into my hands. I smiled at Andras and hid the bag in the folds of my dress as Anya entered the room.

"How was your shopping trip?" I asked my mother politely.

"Always more trouble than it's worth," she said, sighing. "Everything is much too expensive, as usual. I really have to bargain to get what I want." I imagined Anya arguing with a shoe salesman over a few cents. "And I see that you have not touched your lunch," Anya said.

"Oh, I had a stomachache," I said.

I sat at the table and hid the bonbons on my lap while I ate my potatoes. After lunch Andras and I divided the bonbons. There was one left over, which we gave to Colette.

Colette turned out to be better than Mitzi Neni. She didn't say a thing about Maxi leaking sawdust. Some sawdust did come out, but she covered it with the bedspread when she fixed my bed.

The week after Colette arrived, she and Anya spent an hour in the bathroom fixing their hair and putting on makeup. Anya told Colette to cut her hair; it would look more stylish. She offered to pay for the best hairdresser in Budapest.

Anya came out of the bathroom and sat down at the piano. She played Schubert's "Trout" Quintet over and over. When she finally stopped, she folded her hands in her lap, and I could see that there were tears in her eyes. She looked toward the wall. For the first time I thought that maybe Anya and I did have something in common: we both hated that wall. It was all Apa's fault. He was the one who didn't want to live with us. He was the one who had called the workmen secretly while we were away. Anya wiped her eyes with a handkerchief, placed her hands back on the piano keys, and played a simple tune—a children's song I'd learned from Mitzi Neni. Anya sang the words in German. I joined in for the refrain in Hungarian.

Mostly I tried to stay away from Colette, Anya, and Andras by staying in my room with Maxi. We sat together at my desk and practiced writing. First I copied the whole alphabet onto my tablet. Then I practiced writing my full name, *Schnurmacher Maria Etelka Olga*, in all kinds of script. The *Maria* was Apa's choice, I knew. Anya had wanted to name me Miette after a lady in a French romance, but Apa said that in Hungary you could use only a name that belonged to a saint, so they settled on Maria. I tried to imagine them actually talking together, but I couldn't.

Etelka was from my father's mother, who died when Apa was seven. She was the only real Christian in my whole family, and her husband's family hated her because she wasn't Jewish. *Olga* was from my mother's mother, whom I'd also never met. The *Schnurmacher* was the best part because I shared it with Uncle Lipot. Even if he didn't like our name, I did. Besides, the *S* was a fun letter to write. I wrote it in German gothic letters, shadow letters, and block letters.

One day when Colette had been with us for several months, I was in my room practicing my writing. I glanced out the window at the schoolkids going home for lunch and wished again that I was one of them. I'd missed the cut-off date by two weeks. Apa had tried to get the principal to make an exception for me, explaining that I could already read well and spoke three languages, but the principal stuck to the rules. He reminded my father that he had already made enough exceptions for his son. Andras had failed math and my father had convinced the principal to promote him to the next grade anyway, promising that Andras would be tutored in math all summer. But the principal would not make an exception for my birthday that came two weeks too late.

The door of my room opened, and there stood Apa.

"What are you doing here?" I asked him.

"I decided to make a surprise visit," he said, coming over to my desk to see my work. "Marika, who taught you to write so beautifully?"

I shrugged. "Nobody."

He sat next to me and watched me form the letters, up

strokes light, down strokes dark. I breathed in the sweet smell of his cologne. He looked so tall and distinguished in his suit, but the lines around his eyes were deep. He sighed. "Mari, I have to go eat."

"Where?"

"In my apartment."

I was sorry for asking. Of course he would not eat in my apartment, in Anya's apartment. He patted me on the head and I wanted him to leave.

The next morning I found a stack of new books on my desk in German, Hungarian, and French. On the top Apa had written, "For Marika and Maxi to read or copy. Love, Apa."

I decided not to read the French one. I didn't like anything French except bonbons. But the cover had a picture of two children with a map of Europe behind them. The book was called *The Travels of Anne and Julien.* I envied them. Think of it, being able to go wherever you wanted! Apa said I was much too young to travel, but how old did I have to be?

The first page had a picture of the Swiss Alps. Someday I'd go there. I'd ski in the soft snow. I'd sip hot cocoa in a chalet. Reading the French caption was easy. Colette came in and read a chapter out loud to me. At one point the boy in the story, Julien, got stuck climbing out of a window to catch a glimpse of his girlfriend. Colette and I giggled. She said, "I could try to catch a glimpse of my Eric that way."

I tried to imagine Colette with her wide hips fitting through my window and climbing down the rose trellis. Then I closed the book and ran downstairs to find the twins, Tibor and Tamas, who were just walking up the hill from school. They lived on the first floor of our duplex, and their father was Apa's business partner. Tibor and Tamas were three months older than me, so they were already in first grade.

"Want to climb the tree?" I asked them, pointing to the apricot tree in our back yard.

They looked at each other. "We have to practice first," Tibor said. He played the violin.

Tamas nodded. He played the cello. "And then we have to do our homework."

I waited for them in the tree, but they never came out.

That night Colette tiptoed into my room. She checked to make sure I was asleep. I stayed still, shut my eyes, and kept my breathing even, but once I knew her back was to me I opened my eyes. She was trying to squeeze herself through the window. She tried going forward first, but she couldn't reach the trellis. Finally she turned around and made her way down.

I snuck to the window to watch. The trellis held, and the thorns snagged her sleeve only once. When she was near the bottom I saw a shadow. Was that Eric in our yard?

Someone grabbed Colette around the waist and she screamed. In the darkness I saw the stooped back of Andras.

"I'm being kidnapped," shrieked Colette.

Apa came out of his apartment and joined Andras in the rose garden. Colette was crying. Apa was trying to calm her down and get her to go back to bed.

"But Eric is waiting," she said.

"Then Eric will keep on waiting," he said.

I heard her make her way back upstairs, sniffling in the hallway. I heard Apa and Andras talking in the garden. Andras said that we didn't need another nanny. Apa said that my French was still not perfect. He started to say something about how important it was for people to learn everything they could, especially Jews, but Andras stopped him. "I've heard that a million times already," he said. Apa didn't answer.

When the sun was just rising, I fell asleep. By the time I woke up, Colette was already on the train back to Paris, so I never even said good-bye to her. Andras came into my room when the sun was high and told me that everything was taken care of. Colette would not be back. I shrugged my shoulders. It didn't make any difference to me, but Anya would miss Colette, and for that I was sorry.

ANYA

August 1935

No more nannies after Colette. Apa decided that my French was good enough, and Anya said that I was old enough to look after myself. Andras would help when he came home from school. But there was one problem. Anya thought I was still too young to walk to school and back without an adult.

"When school starts in September, I will accompany you both ways," she said.

I imagined standing in front of the school building with Anya. Everyone would stare at the makeup around her eyes and on her lips. Her clothes were too fancy. I'd walked past there many times and I never saw anyone's mother. "I can walk with Tibor and Tamas," I said.

"No, Marika, they are not much older than you are. I will be your chaperone," Anya insisted.

Anya had the dressmaker, Sari Neni, sew me a dress for the first day of school. The fabric was an ugly mustard color, and it had smocking at the top like babies' dresses.

"I will not try it on," I said firmly, crossing my arms over my naked chest so that Sari Neni could not pull the dress over my head.

"Marika, after Sari Neni worked so hard to sew this just for you, the least you can do is try it on."

"That is a dress for babies, and I will not wear it," I repeated loudly to make sure that Anya caught every word.

Anya and Sari Neni tried to lift the dress gingerly over my head, but I ducked and crouched down on the floor. The piano was close by and I eyed my hiding place but decided I was too big to be stuck there for the entire afternoon. Then Anya jerked me by the arm so hard that I was forced to stand up, and in one swift movement Sari Neni pulled the dress over my head. When I struggled, the pins scratched me, so I stood stiffly, my chin up, staring at the ceiling.

"A little tight in the chest," Sari Neni said, pulling at a basting thread. She bent down to adjust the hemline. "Marika, if you don't put your head down, the hem will be crooked."

"So what if it is? I'll never wear it anyway," I said, trying to stamp my right foot but feeling the pins on my thigh.

"You will wear it," Anya said, her face red and so sweaty that her makeup ran down her cheeks. Why was my mother so different from everyone else's? Why did she have layers of lipstick on her lips while everyone else's mother had only a thin line? Anya wiped at her eyes, and the black eyeliner smudged with the blue.

Finally the fitting was over and the mustard-colored fabric was pulled over my head. I ducked under Sari Neni's arms, ran into my room, and hugged Maxi.

"Maxi, I hate that dress," I said. "I won't go to school in a dress for babies." Maxi flopped his head to one side. I lay down on my bed and hugged him against my stomach. My thigh stung from a pin that had scratched me at the last minute. I looked at the thin red line that formed there. Sari Neni was so mean to scratch me with a pin. Then I put Maxi on my pillow, went over to my desk, and picked up the fountain pen Apa had given me.

Sari Neni brought the dress to my room fully hemmed and adjusted to my thick waist. As soon as she left, I spread it out on my desk and held the pen, full of ink, above the fabric. I imagined the ink spilling onto the mustard-colored dress and seeping into the fabric. My arm was sore where Anya had jerked it. She'd never been like that before. Apa would say I was too young to handle ink. I threw the pen across the room and stuffed the dress under my pillow.

I had another idea. I would get sick and not go to school. Mitzi Neni said that if you washed under your arms with soap but didn't rinse off, you would get a terrible red rash. That would be easy, but would a rash keep me home from school? What I really needed was a fever. The best way was to wet my hair and go outside in the wind. That surely brought a fever and tonsillitis. I put my head under the bathroom sink and went out on the small balcony. I leaned as far as I could over the railing to make sure I caught the breeze. There was nothing more to do but wait, so Maxi and I read for a few hours on the balcony.

I had two helpings of paprika chicken at dinner. No sign of a fever. Then, by evening, I started to feel a little swelling in my neck. I looked in the mirror. There was nothing except for the usual mole. Then I took a flashlight and looked into my throat. My tonsils were red with a few little white dots starting. I shut my mouth and smiled. It was Wednesday night, Apa's night to visit.

The door of our apartment opened and I heard Apa's deep voice in the hallway. He went into Andras's room to help him with his homework and stayed there for a long time. I heard Andras stamp his foot.

"How much is fifteen percent of one thousand?" Apa shouted. "Now use your head."

Andras didn't answer.

"It doesn't take a banker to know that," Apa said. "Andras, you have to make an effort to understand."

Still no answer. The door of Andras's room slammed shut. A few minutes later the door of our apartment opened and closed. Andras had gone out.

Apa came to my room. Finally it was my turn, my

favorite time of the week. But I felt dizzy. I looked under my arms. No rash yet, but my cheeks were red and hot.

"Marika, you look sick," Apa said, touching my forehead. "Get into bed."

The room spun in circles. The mustard-colored fabric floated all around me as I felt it with my fingers under my pillow. I would tell everything to Apa—the dress, Anya coming to school with me, the water on my hair. But my throat hurt so much I could not talk, so I just lay on the bed with Maxi and let Apa put cool washcloths on my forehead.

I woke up drenched in sweat but feeling better. The room had stopped spinning. Apa was sitting in a chair in the corner, reading.

"Apa, why are you still here?"

"I wanted to make sure that you were okay." He came over and sat on the edge of my bed.

"It was all my fault," I said. "I got myself sick."

"That is not possible," he said. "You cannot make yourself sick. Germs make you sick. But you did make your mother miserable."

The dress was still bunched up under my pillow. "I hate that ugly color and I don't want Anya to take me to school," I said weakly.

"She is your mother and you must not make her so upset. I'll tell you what. You wear whatever you want, but let your mother accompany you to school. It is important to her. Now, Marika, don't make your mother miserable." Apa looked hard into my eyes. "Your mother has had a hard time already. And there are more hard times to come." He kissed my forehead and said good night. His tall frame filled the doorway. He turned to look at me and said in German, "*Schlafe gut*, sleep well." I didn't answer. He left my room, quietly closing the door behind him.

I stared at the wall. Of course Anya was having a hard time, but that was all his fault. He was the one who built the wall in our apartment. Before that, Anya used to walk around the house humming, but after the wall, she sat at the piano playing the same songs over and over. He was the cause of Anya's misery, not me. It wasn't a mustard-colored baby dress that made Anya cry as she moved her fingers over the piano keys. It wasn't my fault. *More hard times to come*, Apa said. What did he mean? Why were there always so many secrets in our house? Was he planning to build another wall?

I dreamed that all the kids at school pointed at my mother and said she looked like a ghost in her makeup and silk dresses. She stared at their mouths as they talked. They whispered that my mother was a strange phantom. Maybe I was too.

I was sick and missed the first five days of school. Tibor and Tamas brought me the homework from my teacher. I finished it in about five minutes. Maybe first grade would be too easy for me. I would have to go right into second grade with Tibor and Tamas.

Monday my fever was gone and I went to my first day of school wearing an ordinary blue skirt and white blouse. Anya didn't say a thing about going with me. Maybe Apa told her I was old enough, or maybe she was tired of fighting. Tibor walked on one side of me and Tamas on the other. They dropped me off at the first-grade classroom.

SCHOOL

September 1935

Most of the kids in my class didn't even know how to hold a pencil. The teacher spent Monday showing us how to position our fingers. The next morning we made loops on lined paper, and in the afternoon we were supposed to learn the sounds of the letters by acting them out as we said them. The *s* sound was a snake hissing and we had to narrow our eyes and wiggle our tongues. For the *sh* we had to pretend to rock a baby. I read the stories at the end of the primer instead of practicing. Suddenly I heard my name.

"Maria, you do not care to participate with the rest of us?"

I didn't answer.

"Maria, what sound does the snake make?"

I hissed all by myself with thirty-nine pairs of eyes on my mouth.

"Very good. Now how does a snake look?"

I wiggled my tongue.

"Now you will keep up with the class, is that correct?"

I nodded.

On Thursday we had religion class. The priest taught us a Latin phrase, *Dominus vobiscum*, May the Lord be with you. I liked the way the words rolled off his tongue. Apa had a Latin dictionary in his bookcase, so maybe Maxi and I could learn more Latin words. Then I could know exactly what the priest was saying during Sunday mass. The religion classroom had a painting on the wall of Jesus and Mary. The stories in our religion book were more complicated than the ones in our primer.

During gym, I saw Tibor and Tamas in their blue shorts and white shirts playing soccer on the big field. I had to play freeze tag with the girls. My one-piece gym uniform was five sizes too big for me and hung low at the crotch. I watched Tibor score a goal. At the same time a girl tagged me and I was frozen.

"Watching the boys already, at your age," the gym teacher said, shaking her head. I blushed. I wanted to tell her that it was just my neighbor, Tibor, but I looked down at my feet and didn't say anything. The other girls ran all over the field, and nobody came to unfreeze me.

On my way to school the next day I stopped at Apa's apartment. "I don't want to go to school," I told him. "All they do is baby stuff like *Shhhh*." I rocked my imaginary baby.

Apa smiled.

"It's not funny. That's really all they do."

"Only at the beginning. You'll see, all the kids will be reading before you know it."

"I don't think so. They don't even know the alphabet."

"Now you better hurry or you'll be late. Tibor and Tamas are probably waiting for you."

"I'm not going."

Apa's face got stern. "Maria, I've had enough. You have to bear with it. There are lots of things in life we have to bear with. Acting out letter sounds is not the worst thing, especially considering what's going on in the world right now." Apa pointed to the newspaper lying open on his desk. The headline was something about a man named Hitler and the Nazi Party in Germany. But why did Apa care more about what was happening so far away than he did about me? "Now go," Apa said, picking up his newspaper. I ran down the front steps and out of the apartment with the salty taste of tears in my mouth.

"Are you okay?" Tibor asked when he saw me.

I wanted to tell him that I was not okay at all, that school was an awful place, and that not even my own father would believe me. Tamas was ahead, shouting for Tibor to hurry up. "You better go," I said, and my voice cracked.

"Are you sure?" he asked.

I nodded. When Tibor caught up with his brother, I

really started crying. I could turn right at the corner and head away from the school building. Uncle Lipot might be home. He would scoop me in his arms and say, "So how's my girl today?" He would give me chocolate milk and sweet rolls even if it was before lunch. But then he would ask why I wasn't in school. He might even get stern, like Apa. I could just wander around by myself downtown, looking into the windows of the shops. But what if by chance I ran into Anya?

At the corner I turned left. The school building was ahead. Tibor was waiting for me by the entrance. "Mari, are you all right?" he asked, handing me a folded handkerchief. "School gets better after a while," he said. I wiped my eyes and blew my nose. Tamas was calling him, but still he stayed with me. "I mean it. In a few months, you'll be used to it." Tibor squeezed my hand. "Just wait."

In my classroom I took out my book, *The Count of Monte Cristo*. When all the other kids came in, the teacher started her phonics lesson, but I continued to read. She didn't tell me to put my book away. When she called on me for letter sounds, I knew the answers. It wasn't hard for me to read and listen to the teacher at the same time, so I read through the entire afternoon. After a while the girl behind me scooted her chair closer to mine. I scooted forward to get away, but my chair hit the one in front. There was no place to scoot.

"Hey, could you please hold your book a little to the

side so I can see it too?" she whispered. "You're getting to the best part."

I glanced back at her, surprised. I thought everyone else was learning the consonant sounds. The teacher called on me for the *zs* sound. I got it right.

"Can anyone think of a word with this sound?" the teacher asked.

The girl behind me raised her hand. "My name, Zsofi," she said.

"Correct," said the teacher.

Zsofi was waiting for me outside the classroom door after school. Her bright red hair curled around her blue eyes, which practically popped out of her head, especially when she started talking.

"Can you believe we have to do those dumb letter sounds?" she said.

I moved my tongue like a snake and she laughed. We talked the whole way home, about the teacher, the horrible gym uniforms, books we liked. Zsofi knew German and French, just like me. She knew the story of Julien, so I told her about Colette climbing out of my window. She laughed so hard she had to lean on the lamppost to catch her breath. Then I told her that I wanted to learn more Latin phrases.

"Can you teach me one?" Zsofi asked.

"Don't you remember? *Dominus vobiscum*," I said.

Zsofi shook her head. "I don't go to the Catholic religion class," she said.

"Why not?" I asked.

Zsofi looked around. "I'm Jewish," she whispered.

"So where do you go?"

"Nowhere. Because there's no rabbi in the school, I'm supposed to stay in the hall and study my 'Israelite religion.'" Zsofi giggled and took a magazine out of her book bag. "But here's what I study."

I wanted to tell Zsofi that I was Jewish too, and that I'd be happy to join her in the hall, but Apa might be mad. Instead I said, "Then I'll teach you Latin. *Dominus vobiscum* means 'May the Lord be with you.'" Zsofi repeated it perfectly the first time.

At the corner we parted. Zsofi lived over by the small apartments on Krisztina Ut, and I lived up the hill.

"See you tomorrow," I said.

I watched her skip down the street, in a hurry to get home. I wished that my apartment was next door to hers. Then we could walk the whole way home together. We could hold hands and skip at the same time. I would have a small apartment like other kids. I would not have to pass Apa's door. As slowly as I could, I walked up the hill. Anya was waiting for me in the front hallway.

"Mari, where have you been? I was just going out to find you. I will have to start accompanying you as I planned," she said anxiously.

What could I say? That I was in no hurry to get home? That I came home as slowly as I could? Anya's eyes were red. Was she really that worried? She glanced toward the wall and then back to me.

"It will be nice to walk home together," she said gently.

"Tomorrow I will hurry home," I said. "I promise." Then I went into my room, shut the door, and lay on my bed with Maxi for a long time. What would Zsofi say if she saw my mother waiting for me after school in her blue silk dress with the gold necklace? She would think that I was a rich, spoiled kid with a crazy mother, that's what she would think. I would hurry home. Anya would forget all about meeting me.

On my desk I found a Latin dictionary and a new novel called *Little Lord Fauntleroy*, with a note from Apa. "Thought you might enjoy these, Love, Apa." Apa had a way of knowing things that I never told him. But then he also had a way of not telling me things that I wanted to know. I looked over at the wall and imagined Apa's shoes lined up on the other side. His suits would be hanging in the closet. I thought of Zsofi's chatter about her mother, her father, her two older brothers. A normal, ordinary family. I reread Apa's note. I would write him back that I didn't want the gifts. Apa thought that if he gave me gifts, everything would be okay. I imagined the words flowing from my pen: *Dear Apa, thanks but no thanks. Marika.* No, *Maria.* That was my real name, the one he had given me. The cover of

Little Lord Fauntleroy showed a beautiful boy with blond ringlets. I hugged Maxi tight and opened the book. Tomorrow I'd pass it on to Zsofi—that is, if she hadn't already read it.

Sore Throats

November 1938

I got a sore throat often in primary school. The doctor said he hoped I would outgrow it, but even in third grade I missed the first two weeks of school. Zsofi said she never heard of anybody getting sick so often. Anya said it was because I was stubborn and never listened to anyone. If I ate my spinach like a good girl, I would be healthy. The cook said the problem was that I drank cold water when I was sweaty. If I didn't run around all afternoon with those awful boys, Tibor and Tamas, and get totally out of breath and drenched in sweat, the sore throats would be gone. The cook tried not letting me play with the boys, but unless she actually locked the door, she could not keep me in.

Andras said that Tibor and Tamas were spoiled brats, and just because they were twins and good in music was no reason for them to act like the top of the world. To me they were the perfect neighbors. We played leapfrog and climbed the apricot tree in the back yard. The most fun was when we pretended to be triplets. They had an extra pair of leather shorts for me. I put my hair under one of their hats and stood between the twins. "My name is Tivi. I'm your long-lost brother from..."

"Where should you be from?" Tamas asked.

I said the first thing that came into my mind. "Galicia."

"Galicia? Where's that?"

I shrugged. "I'm not sure."

"Yes, our long-lost brother from Galicia who got separated from us at birth and raised by a wicked step-mother," Tibor said.

"Yes, and when she got mad, she let the chickens peck at my eyes," I said, thinking of the worst punishment I could imagine.

"Let's not make her that bad," Tibor said.

"Well, anyway, you ran away from your wicked step-mother and found your way back to us," Tamas said. Tamas and Tibor hugged me at once, one on either side.

"Tibor, Tamas, time to come in and practice." Their father, Leo Bacsi, was calling from the window.

The boys looked at each other. "Better hurry," Tibor said.

They ran quickly through the back door, and I was abandoned in the garden wearing leather shorts and a boy's hat. The notes of the scale on the violin and the cello came from the open window. "Slow down!" Leo Bacsi shouted. "Can't you hear, that is much too fast. Tibor, what is the matter with your ears?"

I went in to Maxi. "Maxi, what is the matter with your ears?" I repeated, mimicking their father. Then I sat at my desk and practiced my writing. Up strokes light, down strokes dark, slow and even. I lifted up my pen and took a breath. I wrote *Little Lord* ... but then instead of *Fauntleroy*, I wrote *Schnurmacher*. I would love to be an English orphan with blond ringlets and rosy cheeks. Then I could live in an orphanage with Tibor and Tamas. As I was writing, I felt the familiar tickle in my throat. I swallowed hard a few times, but it didn't go away.

"Here it goes again," I told Maxi.

By evening my throat was swollen and I was in bed with the washcloth on my forehead. The doctor came and examined me. Afterward, he and Apa talked for a long time in the hallway. Uncle Lipot was there too. "Hitler's Nazi army has marched into Austria," I heard the doctor say. I tried to listen, but the noises of the street below muffled the words. I dozed off, then woke when Apa came into my room.

"Marika, you will be going to Vac for the whole summer." He tried to sound cheerful. "The country air is the only way to get rid of these persistent sore throats."

"The whole summer?" I asked suspiciously.

Apa nodded. "Six weeks. Doctor's orders."

"But the doctor was talking about Hitler, not about my throat."

"Marika, the doctor is not to be disputed."

"Can I go to Switzerland with Andras instead?" I asked. Andras was going to spend the summer in the Swiss Alps studying for his exams.

Apa shook his head. "Marika, how will your brother be able to study if you are there to distract him? Be patient. When you are older we'll travel together. But for now you must listen to the doctor. I'll tell you what. How about you invite your friend Zsofi to stay with you?"

Zsofi didn't even know we had a summer house. If she did, her eyes would open wide and she would say, *Marika, your family has everything,* the way she did when she saw my father's new car. "No," I answered quickly.

"Wouldn't it be better to have some company?" he asked. "And for Zsofi it would be such a treat, so much better than a hot apartment right in the heart of the city all summer long. She could even have her own bedroom there, imagine."

"No," I said again, louder. "It would not be better. Zsofi's apartment is just fine. Maybe I should stay there with *her* for the summer. She never gets a sore throat."

"Now, Maria, calm down," Apa said, trying to get me to lie back on the fluffy feather pillows.

"Zsofi doesn't need her own bedroom. The best part of her day is at night when she and her brothers tell stories in the dark."

Apa stood up. "As you like, Maria. But it will be Vac

for you this summer, with Zsofi or without."

"How about Tibor and Tamas—can they come?"

This time Apa answered quickly. "No. You need to find company other than those boys." Then he was gone.

I fell asleep imagining myself on a train through the mountains in the Alps.

The last day of school Zsofi asked me if I could stop at her house on the way home. Her mother had a special treat for us. I told her I had to go to Vac for the summer because of my sore throats, but I didn't say anything about her joining me. She said she was going to help her father in the tailor's shop.

"Do what?" I asked.

"Sew, I guess," she said, rolling her eyes. I laughed. In the domestic skills class, Zsofi was the absolute worst. I tried to teach her how to do the edge stitch around the white handkerchief the way the teacher showed us, but the fabric bunched up and the thread got tangled. Finally I stuck her handkerchief in my book bag and finished it at home.

"How on earth are you going to help your father sew?" I asked.

Zsofi shrugged. "There must be something in the shop I can do."

We entered her building through the back and went past three doors before coming to Zsofi's. Her mother looked older than I'd imagined, thin like Zsofi but without the red hair.

"Oh, Marika, come in, come in," she said. "Zsofi does nothing but talk about you." She took both my hands in hers. "Now sit down and have some palacsinta pancakes and cocoa."

Zsofi and I sat on a little bench. Her mother sat across from us. The kitchen was smaller than the bathroom at my house. Small pots of flowers were blooming on the windowsill. As soon as my plate was empty, Zsofi's mother gave me another palacsinta rolled up with walnuts and sugar. Her face was kind and simple. I thought about the way Anya stared at people when they talked, watching their mouths but missing much of what they said.

When it was time for me to go, Zsofi wished me a good summer.

"Same to you," I said quietly.

As I started up the hill toward my house, Zsofi called after me. "Skip rocks in the river for me. Skip one ten times on my tenth birthday."

I nodded. "I'll try."

I thought of Apa's suggestion. Invite Zsofi to Vac. But all I said was, "You better practice that running stitch." Then I turned the corner.

Wednesday night I heard the front door open. I wondered where Anya went while Apa was visiting us. Did she go to her father's? She had no friends, really. Did she wander the streets like Andras? I didn't even look up when Apa came into my room. I kept right on working on my story about Little Lord Schnurmacher, covering my paper so he wouldn't see it. The ink smeared.

"How was your last day of school?" Apa asked.

"Fine."

"I heard you went to Zsofi's house after school."

I nodded.

"Maybe when you get back from Vac, you should invite Zsofi over to our house," he said.

I didn't answer.

"You know, if somebody invites you, you really must invite them back. I already talked to the cook about it. She will fix dobos torta, how about that?"

I shook my head.

"Oh, does Zsofi not like torta? Well, we can make cookies then."

I heard the irritability in Apa's voice, as if I were an ungrateful brat. I wished he'd leave so I could recopy the page I'd ruined. I was thinking about how I'd spend the summer in Vac working on *Little Lord Schnurmacher*, and then when school started again I could give it to Zsofi. I could just imagine her face as she read it, smiling, blue eyes popping out.

Apa cleared his throat. I was in for a lecture. "Maria, you must not be afraid of what others might think of you.

You must not be ashamed because we have more and Zsofi has less. This has nothing to do with anything."

"But I hate all this!" I shouted, pointing to the Persian rug on the floor and the chandelier hanging from the ceiling. "And if it has nothing to do with anything, can't you just take it all out of my room?" Once I got started, I couldn't stop. The meaner the better. "And you can get rid of the car, and the summer house at Vac." I stopped to take a breath. "And that too," I said pointing at the wall between his apartment and ours.

Apa sighed. "There is a threat of war. I know you think it is far away, but Hungary may be involved someday too, and you have nothing else to worry about but chandeliers and walls? I suppose that is a good thing. You are only a child."

Apa left. I felt stupid, like a selfish baby. *Only a child,* he had said. I was eleven years old. If he told me what was going on, maybe I wouldn't be such a baby. If he didn't keep everything a secret until it was too late. Until it was already over. I tried to imagine my house before the wall, but I couldn't remember how it had looked.

Andras came into my room and sat on the edge of my bed. "I'll send you postcards from Switzerland," he said.

"Thanks."

"I'll bring you some Swiss chocolate too, the kind with pretty pictures of chalets and mountains on them. You like milk chocolate best, right?"

I nodded.

"You're lucky, Marika. You get to play in the river while I have to study math for the whole summer."

I thought of the river at Vac with its clear water flowing over shiny stones, and suddenly I was glad I would be there. Andras showed me how to flick my wrist so the rocks would skip lightly over the water.

"Choose round, flat rocks and wet them first," he advised.

"Okay."

"Uncle Lipot will probably visit you in Vac. Anyway, you're lucky to be away from Apa and his lectures and his lady friends."

"Lady friends? What do you mean?" I asked.

Andras blushed. "You are too young to understand," he said.

So Andras thought I was a baby too. Nobody ever really talked to me. Nobody except Zsofi. Six weeks would seem like a very long time.

THE SUMMER HOUSE

June 1939

The next morning I laid out a few things to take to Vac. I put my ink, pen, and notebook for *Little Lord Schnurmacher* on my desk. What about Maxi? In the past he'd always come with me to Vac, but this time I hesitated.

"Will you be too bored there, Maxi, with nothing to do all day long?" I hugged him tight. "Maybe you better stay here to protect my room. Don't let in any workmen." I tousled his hair and sat him up on the bed. He smiled back at me as if my decision to leave him home as a watchman suited him very well indeed. I buckled the suitcase.

"Did you ask Anya to pack you a nice skirt and blouse?" Apa asked me.

I looked up, surprised. Tall as he was, he had such a light step that I never heard him coming. "I don't need that at Vac."

"But you will at Kekes."

"Kekes? What do you mean?"

"I mean that from Vac you will take a bus to Kekes for a one-week vacation on top of the mountain."

"By myself?"

"Uncle Lipot will put you on the bus in Vac, and I'll be there at Kekes to meet you. Then for the week it's just you and me, hiking and swimming."

I stood up and hugged Apa as hard as I could. It had been such a long time since I'd hugged him, but the smell of his cologne was always the same.

"Where will we stay?"

"At the Kekes Hotel, right at the peak of the mountain," Apa said. "So, Marika, tell Anya you need a skirt and blouse. Now I had better get to my office. See you at the summit," he said, waving to me from the doorway.

"At the summit," I repeated. "Maxi, I really am going to travel. To a real mountain." I opened the book about Anne and Julien to look more closely at the picture of the Alps. Of course Kekes was not the Alps, but a mountain was a mountain, even if it was in Hungary. "Someday, Maxi, we'll travel far away from here." I looked at the map of Europe printed in the front of the book and traced my finger through Yugoslavia to Italy, and then even farther to the edge of the map. "Someday."

On Friday my mother got a telegram from her cousin. He and his wife and their small son would be passing through Budapest and wanted to spend a night with us. Anya was in a total tizzy. She didn't like anything that upset her plans. She complained to the maids that she had nowhere for three extra people to sleep. What would Anya do if she had to live in Zsofi's small apartment with three cots in one room? Andras said that no two-year-old brat was going to share his room, even for a few nights. Finally we decided that the boy would sleep in my room in my old crib that was still stored up in the attic. His parents would sleep in the storage room, which the maids were frantically trying to clean.

We wouldn't leave for Vac for a few days. It wasn't very often that we had visitors from another country. They were Austrian, so I brushed up on my German greetings. Then I found an old train set in the attic and assembled it for the little boy, Georg.

Their train was two hours late. Anya was upset because the small sandwiches she had asked the cook to prepare got stale. Finally the doorbell rang. The man and his wife seemed nervous, but the child was cheerful and friendly. I took his hand. "Mari," he said with a German *r*, and he hugged me around the legs.

I took Georg to my room and showed him the train. He kept saying "choo choo" and pointing to the engine as it whizzed around. Then I read him a short German book about Struwwel Peter, a little boy who refused to comb his hair or cut his fingernails. Georg listened with his big eyes wide open and his thumb in his mouth. After a while he started yawning, and we played with Maxi until Georg got so tired that he lay down on the floor and fell asleep. I picked him up, kissed the top of his head, and put him gently into the crib. If he were my own baby brother, we could play every day. I put Maxi into the crib with Georg.

I could hear my mother, my grandfather, and Georg's parents talking in low voices from the living room. They were whispering. Georg's father said that they should be quiet because I might not be asleep yet. I tiptoed to the doorway so I could hear better. "I was arrested on my way to work," Georg's father said.

"What were you doing?" my grandfather asked.

"Walking. Simply walking to work."

"And they stopped you in the street?"

"They held a gun to my back and marched me into the office of the SS."

"That can't be," Anya said. "Civilized people don't just arrest someone for no reason. Could it be that they mixed you up with someone else?"

"You must try to understand," Georg's father said. "The situation is not what you imagine at all. People are arrested for being Jews, only for being Jews. They took me along with some other Jewish men to the headquarters of the SS. They told us all to line up against the wall with our arms up. We heard them take their pistols out of their pockets. Then they fired, and at the same time the soldiers quickly pulled the rug that we were standing on. We crumpled to the ground, thinking that we had been shot. I just lay there on the floor thinking about my little Georg and how I would never see him again. Next thing I heard was laughter, loud laughter and glasses clinking. The officers were having a drink while we thought we were dead on the floor. They had fired over our heads. 'Would you like to play again?' they asked. We sat up, and they let us crawl out the door like dogs."

Anya was crying. Georg's father went on. "You do not know what is happening in Vienna. The Jews are being rounded up and forced like slaves to wash the stones in the street. I saw one man stop to get a drink. The officer hit him with the back of his rifle and he fell down dead on the wet stones." Georg's father cleared his throat. "Jews are being taken to camps."

"Where?" my grandfather asked.

"In Germany," Georg's father said. His voice faded almost to a whisper. "And from there they will never come back."

"I don't believe it," Anya said.

"Believe it or don't believe it, as you please. But we are leaving. The West does not welcome us, so we are heading East through Romania and across the Black Sea."

"We are taking our chances," Georg's mother said.

"But where will you end up?" my grandfather asked.

I couldn't hear the answer. My legs were cramped under me. I stood up and stretched. My grandfather heard the sound and glanced my way. I hid behind the door for a little while and then I tiptoed to my room.

Georg stirred in his sleep. I patted his head. From my window I looked down at the street. Everything was quiet. The street lamps flickered. A lady and a man walked slowly toward the corner. Maybe they were husband and wife. She took his arm. What were those camps like? Why did Georg's father say that people did not come back? Anyway, those camps were far away. Nothing like that could ever happen in Budapest.

I listened to Georg breathing, and I thought that I heard gun shots far away. It was only the factory down the hill belching its smokestack.

Suddenly I wanted Zsofi to come with me to Vac. On the way we could talk about what Georg's father had said. Zsofi would know what to think. I had never told Zsofi about my Jewish grandparents, but she seemed to know anyway. She always said *we* when she meant *the Jews*. I wished I could stay in the hall with her instead of going to the Catholic religion class. We could read magazines together. We would laugh at the same jokes. Maybe I'd ask Apa if I could stay with Zsofi next year. Finally, long after midnight, I fell asleep.

When I woke up, the sun was streaming into my room. Georg and Maxi were deep in a German conversation. I kept my eyes closed for a few minutes and listened. Georg was telling Maxi all about the trains on the floor. After breakfast, Georg and his parents got ready to leave. Georg kept hugging me around my knees and asking his parents where they were going and if he could stay with me. His parents said they were heading for a long adventure, and that they hoped to end up someday in either Australia or America.

"But I don't like America," Georg said. "I like Marika."

I watched them until they were almost out of sight, his blond curls just a yellow speck.

At the last minute I decided to take Maxi to Vac after all.

I pushed the big chair in the front room of our summer house closer to the window and started reading a book about Admiral Byrd and explorations in Antarctica. I would love to be an explorer like that someday, to be the very first person in the whole world to go somewhere, I thought. I looked closely at an illustration of sled dogs romping in the snow. Maybe there would be snow on top of Kekes. Not enough for dog sleds because it wasn't as high as the Alps, but maybe there would be a few snowy patches left over from the winter.

"Marika, go out and play," the maid said to me. "Your parents sent you here for fresh air and exercise, not to sit inside and read. Now go."

I closed my book and stretched. Play what? Outside the

sun was bright. I walked across the dirt road in my bare feet, stopping at the well for a drink. Apa bought the property for its well. The water came from a very deep underground spring. Suddenly I missed Apa's deep voice and the smell of his cologne even on his weekend clothes. Only four more days until our special trip. Only four more days until I got to see Uncle Lipot. That meant the date of my trip was July sixth. Zsofi's birthday. Hadn't she told me to skip a rock ten times for her on her tenth birthday? I would have to practice.

I went over to the riverbank and looked for round, flat stones. I found a small one and flicked my wrist as I threw it across the water. It skipped three times. Not bad, but not enough. I tried again with a slightly heavier rock. The sun was warm on my back and the cool water felt good on my feet.

Farther down the bank, three boys were also skipping rocks. I watched how they drew their arms way back before throwing the stones. Why were boys always stronger than girls? I thought of Tibor and Tamas. Tamas was stronger than Tibor, but both of them could run faster than me. The three boys had their shirts off and I could see the muscles ripple in their backs. Something stung my shin. I thought it was a wasp, but I heard laughter. Another rock landed like a bomb in front of me.

"Dirty Jew!" one of them yelled.

"I'll get her this time," another one said.

I stepped back just in time and ran across the street to my yard. The maid was hanging clothes on the line. She smiled at me. "Did you have a nice time?" she asked. "It's good to see you playing for a change."

I didn't answer. I still had one of the smooth skipping rocks in my hand. I wanted to go back and skip it for Zsofi. The stone was heavy in my tightly clenched fingers. *Dirty Jew.* How did they know? The sign that said *Schnurmacher* by the mailbox? My black hair? Plenty of Catholic kids in my class had black hair. What about blond-haired, blue-eyed Georg? Would people throw rocks at him and call him a dirty Jew? I remembered the story his father had told. The officers laughed when they pulled out the rug. The boys laughed when the stone hit my shin.

I felt the smooth rock with my thumb. I could go back and hurl that rock at them, hit them in the face, make their noses bleed. But there were three of them and one of me. If Andras were here, he could beat them up in a minute, but he was eating chocolate and drawing triangles in the Alps.

KEKES

July 1939

Uncle Lipot came to Vac a day early. I showed him my story about Little Lord Schnurmacher, and he laughed at all the right places.

"You'll be a writer someday," he said.

"I don't think so," I said, trying to imagine myself at a small desk every day. "An explorer would be more exciting."

"An explorer who writes," he said.

The day with Uncle Lipot was long. He asked me if I wanted to walk along the riverbank, but I remembered the three boys and shook my head. He took me to a small restaurant for lunch. We sat by the window and watched the people going by on their way to market. Uncle Lipot was unusually quiet. He picked at his paprika potatoes and said he was full. I wasn't hungry either, so the two of us sat in the coolness of the restaurant, staring out the window. Three kids went by arm in arm. They were laughing, heads together. I wished I were going home to Tibor and Tamas instead of to Kekes. Uncle Lipot shook his head.

"What's the matter?" I asked.

"Oh, sorry, Marika, nothing is the matter. It's a nice day here by the river, isn't it?"

"But why were you shaking your head?"

"Oh, Marika, I am just wondering how long Hungary will hold out."

"Hold out?"

"Germany has already occupied Austria, and Hungary could be next."

"What do you mean, 'occupied'?"

"That means the army of one country comes in and takes over another." Uncle Lipot bent his head low. "The problem is, I'm afraid the Hungarians will welcome the Germans with open arms, as the Austrians did."

The door of the restaurant opened and a boy came in with his mother. His face looked familiar. He was the smallest of the three boys who had thrown the rocks at me. His mother bought him a roll, and they left.

"Uncle Lipot?" I whispered.

"Hmm?"

"Why does everyone hate the Jews?"

Uncle Lipot put his hand on mine. "Really they are just jealous because so often the Jews are more successful than they are."

I thought about what happened at the riverbank. I was

jealous because they were boys. They had strong muscles in their arms, so their rocks skipped better than mine. "I don't think that could be the reason," I said to Uncle Lipot. Then I told him what had happened on the riverbank.

Uncle Lipot sighed. "You are right. Those boys were not jealous. They were just repeating what they heard from their parents. Oh, Marika, I'm sorry we cannot protect you from everything," he said, forcing a smile. "Tomorrow you will go to Kekes to see Apa."

Uncle Lipot hugged me tight at the small bus station in Vac. "Marika, I think you may still be too young to travel alone," he teased. "How about I buy another ticket and sit right here next to you?"

I smiled and played along. "I don't think so, Uncle Lipot, because my snack is not big enough for two." I knew how much my uncle liked to eat, and one salami sandwich and an apple wouldn't be enough.

"You have a point, Marika," he said. "I guess I'll just have to go home to see what Aunt Ila has fixed for me this afternoon."

The stationmaster yelled "All aboard!" as if the bus were a train going across Europe. It was just a small commuter bus that went up the mountainside, but his voice was the same.

"Have a great time," Uncle Lipot shouted.

"I will," I shouted back.

I took a seat by the window so I could wave to him as the bus pulled away. I knew he was anxious to go home, but he stayed at the station until I could no longer see his waving hand. For a minute I wished that he had come with me. Maybe I *was* too young to travel alone. I looked around at the other passengers sitting near me. They looked like vacationers, carrying picnic baskets and backpacks. The lady sitting closest to me offered me a pastry.

"No thank you," I said. I was under strict orders not to accept things from strangers. She shrugged. I wondered if she thought I was a Jew. Uncle Lipot said people were jealous of the Jews, but why would this lady be jealous of me? I was jealous of Zsofi because she had an ordinary family with a kind mother who served sweet rolls. I was jealous of Tibor and Tamas because their birthday came before mine and they could always beat me when we raced. But who would be jealous of me?

I tried to scoot even closer to the window, but there wasn't much room. I opened my lunch bag and took out the salami sandwich on thick bread. The lady watched me gobble down the whole thing, and the apple too. She shrugged again. I wished that at Kekes Apa and I would be the only vacationers. Who knew about all these other people on the bus? Maybe they would throw stones at me and at Apa too. I wanted to take Maxi out of my bag, but if I did, people would think I was a baby.

The bus was noisy and rattled me back and forth against the window. The salami sandwich felt like lead in my stomach. I might throw up. What would the lady sitting next to me think then? I put my forehead against the cool glass and tried to sleep. Andras was already in Switzerland. I wondered if the Alps looked the way they did in pictures. Was there really snow on them even in summer? What would I do if Apa wasn't waiting for me at the top of the mountain? Uncle Lipot had given me some money, but would it be enough to take the bus back down? Vac was just a gray smudge in the distance. I dozed off and dreamed about rocks skipping across the river, nine, ten, twenty times. The boys on the bank were surprised that I could skip rocks like that. They asked me to show them how.

The bus lurched to a stop. My neck was stiff and I felt dizzy. People around me stood and smoothed out their clothing. I made my way toward the door of the bus. Apa stood on the platform, his arms outstretched, by far the tallest and most distinguished-looking person there. I stumbled down the stairs into his arms.

"Marika, you are so grown up, traveling all this way alone," he said. "How was your journey?"

"Fine, except for the salami sandwich."

"I thought salami was your favorite," he said.

"It was, until now."

"Well, never mind, we'll have chicken from now on,

how about that?" he said. I smiled as we walked arm in arm toward the hotel. "You've grown since I last saw you. I think it will fit," he added.

"What will fit?"

"You'll see," he answered.

The hotel lobby had a high ceiling with a big chandelier in the middle. Our room had a small balcony with a view of the lake. On my bed was a navy blue velvet dress with white piping down the side and a low waist, the kind of dress older girls wore.

"It's beautiful," I said, holding the velvet up to my face. I tried it on and walked slowly around the room so Apa could see. The fit was perfect. Apa took my hand and together we walked to the dining hall. He introduced me to three people at the table. He seemed to know them already, although none of them was familiar to me. One of them told Apa that he certainly looked happier than he had for the past few days.

"Past few days?" I asked Apa. "When did you get here?"

"Oh, a week ago or so," he said.

I was quiet as I picked at the chicken. My stomach still didn't feel completely right. The adults at the table were talking about the possibility of war in Hungary.

"Hungary will keep its independence," said the man to my right.

"How can you be so sure?" said the man across from him.

"Well, we've managed quite well so far," said the first man.

"But for how long?" Apa asked.

It had been nice at Vac not to hear a thing about Germany and Hitler and occupation. Why had Apa gone to Kekes a whole week before me? Wasn't this our special vacation? What did he do there for a whole week alone? I listened again to the adults. One of them asked about the missus.

"Oh, she is back in Budapest," Apa said. "She has things to attend to back home."

"Marika, eat your dinner," Apa said.

I took another bite, but my stomach was unsettled. *The missus*, the man had said. Anya could not have come with Apa, but for a just a second I wondered if it was possible, if the wall in my apartment was gone, if there had been another renovation.

"So you are Marika," one of the men said to me. He was younger than my father, with a head full of bushy hair. "Your father has been raving about you nonstop for a whole week. You are the apple of his eye, you know," he said.

I tried to concentrate on what he was saying.

"Mari, what do you want to be when you grow up? A stockbroker like your father or an actor like me?"

His face looked sincere, as if he really cared. "I'll be a scientist like Madame Curie or an explorer like Admiral Byrd," I said.

"Wonderful choices," he said. Then he asked me all about Madame Curie and Admiral Byrd. By the end of the meal, my chicken was gone and I felt full of ideas. He said that the next time he was in a play in Budapest, he'd send me and Apa tickets for front-row seats.

When we got back to our hotel room, I read Apa my story about Little Lord Schnurmacher.

"Marika, you have a real way with words," he said, "and beautiful penmanship to go with it. Have you thought about becoming a writer?"

"That's just what Uncle Lipot asked me, and the answer is no. A scientist or an explorer," I said decisively. "I can always write about my new discoveries or the places I've explored."

Apa smiled. "Now, Marika, it is late. Get into your pajamas. We have a busy day ahead of us tomorrow."

I took one last look in the mirror before slipping the velvet dress off over my head. I would wear it again when we went to the theater to see Apa's actor friend in the play. I folded it neatly and laid it on the chair next to my bed. The white piping was still visible in the dark room and I fell asleep touching the velvet.

Apa and I put on our swimsuits under our clothes, took our fishing poles, and hiked to a nearby stream. We cast our lines, and in just a few minutes I had a bite.

"Looks like a big trout," Apa said, holding the

flopping fish in his hand and taking it off the hook. My stomach turned and I looked away.

"What's wrong? You eat chicken and pork, don't you?" Apa said.

"But I don't kill it," I said.

"Don't forget, the butcher does," Apa said, slitting the fish skillfully down its middle.

"What I hate is the eye looking at me," I said.

"Then don't look back," Apa said. We made a small fire to cook the trout. Apa gave me the best part right in the middle. "Even better than the one I caught last week," he said. He seemed sorry he'd said anything about last week, but it was too late. I was tired of pretending not to hear.

"Why did you come for a week without me? I could have come from Vac earlier," I said.

"I just needed a vacation," he said lamely.

"You mean this isn't a vacation?" I asked.

"That is not at all what I mean." Then he was quiet, searching for the right words but not finding them. Funny how Apa was so good with words when he explained math to Andras but stuttering now. He sighed. "Sorry. I should have told you long ago. I came with a lady friend."

I remembered Andras using the same term. *Lady friend.*

"Who?" I asked.

Apa didn't say anything for a while. I thought he might try to change the subject, or tell me that I was too young to know everything. But this time I would not give in.

"Sari Neni," he said quietly.

"Sari Neni?" I asked. I knew two ladies named Sari Neni. One was the dressmaker. The other was Tibor and Tamas's mother. "Which Sari Neni?" I whispered. I already knew the answer.

"Tibor and Tamas's mother," he said.

I dropped my fish sandwich onto the pebbles. She lived on the first floor of our house, but I didn't see her often except when she called the boys in to practice their instruments or on her way to the opera. She was an opera singer. Sometimes I heard her singing along with the piano or the violin. She was tall and slender and beautiful, the opposite of Anya with her hunched back. I wanted to go home, to leave this mountaintop, to see Anya, to climb the apricot tree in the back yard with Tibor and Tamas. I felt a lump rising in my throat, but I would not let myself cry, not on top of a mountain with Apa.

"Does Anya know?" I whispered.

Apa nodded. The fish head fell to the ground and lay on its side with one eye staring up. "There is another thing I should tell you. When you get home, your grandfather will be living in my apartment. I got another apartment down the street on Fenyo Utca. It would be better for your mother if I am a little farther away."

"It would be better for my mother if you had never built the wall," I said quietly.

I stood up and walked by myself to the shore of the lake. The water was ice cold but the air was warm. The sun felt hot on my back. I slipped off my outer clothes, took a deep breath, and plunged in. I swam for a long time. Apa called to me to swim closer to shore, but I ignored him. Didn't he know I was a strong swimmer? He'd taught me to swim in the Danube when I was only four years old. Everyone said I was like a little fish. The water was smooth. If I cried in the water, no one would know. I alternated breaststroke and backstroke. The water was wonderful. Apa called. I swam on. The opposite shore was closer. I put my head under and kept going.

When I felt short of breath, I floated on my back. Floating was effortless for me. Zsofi failed swim tests because she couldn't float. She was dense like a rock. Not me. I could stay on top forever. In the water I was as strong as Tibor and Tamas and the boys who threw the rocks. The sky was a clear blue with no clouds. I could float until I fell asleep.

The water felt colder and colder. I treaded furiously for a few minutes to try to get warm, but still I felt frozen, not just on my skin but all the way into my bones. A wave covered my head. Water went into my mouth and nose. I couldn't breathe. I was choking. I thrashed my arms and legs, anything to get the water out, to see the sky. Another wave and I choked again.

. . .

Apa was pounding on my back. When he stopped I opened my eyes and saw the wooden boards of a boat. My throat was completely dry. Apa handed me a small cup of water. I took a sip and threw up.

"Marika, Marika," Apa said over and over again. "My dear Marika."

I turned over on my back and shut my eyes. To talk seemed impossible. Anyway, what could I say? That I was trying to drown?

Apa's actor friend was rowing the boat. "You were too far, even for an explorer," he said. Their voices faded in and out. When we got to shore, they carried me all the way to the hotel room and laid me down on the bed. I didn't move until morning.

At breakfast, Apa said he was sorry that I got so upset about Sari Neni. I took tiny bites of my roll. I didn't even look at Apa's face. If he was really so sorry, then why didn't he take the wall down and move back in with us? Would it be so hard?

The next day we took the train home to Budapest. Apa tried to talk with me, but I answered in monosyllables. Yes, no, no. It was mean, but I couldn't stop myself. Apa finally gave up and read his newspaper.

"Looks bad," he mumbled. "Hitler got half of Poland. I wonder what he'll get next?"

"Can I see another page of the newspaper?" I asked.

From the station in Budapest we took the streetcar

toward our house and then walked up the hill. Apa carried both of our suitcases until we got to the corner. Then he handed me mine.

"Anya will be happy to see you," he said. "My address is number 4 Fenyo Utca. Right there, the one with the balcony." He pointed down the street.

I nodded.

He turned left and I kept going straight. I looked back once, and Apa was watching me. He waved.

"Thanks. Thanks for the vacation," I shouted.

SHOES

September 1939

Anya told me to squeeze my feet into my shoes, but my toes were all curled up. "If you hadn't gone barefoot all summer long, your feet would not have spread wide like an elephant's," she said. Then she dragged me off to the shoe store, grumbling the whole way about how my father had plenty of money for his own elegant suits and gifts for his "friend," but never enough for his own children.

Inside the shoe store I picked out a pair of loafers. "No, Mari, you need tie shoes. Loafers will only encourage your feet to spread more." Anya picked out a pair of black-and-white tie shoes that were slightly cheaper.

"I won't wear those," I said.

"Then what will you wear?"

"My old shoes."

"But you can't even squeeze your feet into them."

"Then I'll go barefoot," I said, hiding my feet under the chair.

"May I help you?" asked the salesman.

"Yes," Anya said, clearing her throat. "My daughter would like these shoes here, but they are far too expensive." She held up the black-and-white shoes.

The man looked at my mother's made-up face and gold earrings. For a moment I wondered if he might throw a rock. "The prices have gone up lately, Madame, especially on imported leather. These shoes are made of the finest cowhide in all of Italy."

My mother looked convinced for a moment. "Well, how about adding some extra laces and polish for that price?" she asked.

"I really shouldn't, but since you are an old customer, I suppose it can be done."

Anya smiled. This was her prize moment, when she found herself a bargain. I wanted to run out of the store. Couldn't Anya see that the salesman was just humoring her? What difference did laces or polish make to him?

Anya counted out the cash slowly. "Don't forget those laces," she said.

The assistant nodded, irritated, and thrust the package toward me. I saw him roll his eyes as we turned to leave. Just as we were opening the door, he mumbled, "Rich Jew."

I jerked my head up. Anya hadn't heard the stinging words. She couldn't even hear when you were three feet from her face. I thought of the boys at Vac. I wished for smooth river rocks to throw at all of them, at the sales assistant, the boys at Vac, at Anya, and Apa too.

"I'm sorry, Mari," Anya said apologetically. "I know these shoes aren't your first choice, but I have to look out for your feet. I'll tell you what. If your father agrees, I'll buy you a pair of dress shoes too, just for special occasions."

Anya's makeup was running. Sweat had gathered on her forehead. Her hair, usually so neatly arranged around her ears, was hanging loose. I hated Apa for what he had done to her. I hated myself for wanting the loafers instead, but the next time I would do the same thing. I couldn't stop myself.

Anya chattered about how school was about to start. Now I had new shoes, but I still needed a few dresses. Sari Neni would come soon to measure me. I wondered if she would call us rich Jews too. Everybody in the whole city of Budapest knew that the Schnurmacher family was Jewish. Someday I would go far away from our house and the wall Apa built and the boys who threw rocks and everyone who knew us, and then I would change my name.

Sari Neni came bright and early. "My goodness, you are getting a little on the chubby side," she said, pinching my cheeks.

It was true. All that sitting around at Vac and I couldn't fit into any of my old clothes.

"You better watch her weight," Sari Neni said to my

mother as she pulled the tape measure around my waist. "Bigger than mine," she said, jotting *65 centimeters* into her notebook. "The sleeves will have to be extra long. She has long arms and big hands. Big flat feet too," she added.

"You are not sewing socks, are you?" I asked.

She ignored my comment.

I stood on the dining room table and Sari Neni measured the distance from my waist to my knees. She brought a partially sewn dress that I tried on so she could check the hemline. I felt a pin in my thigh.

"Ouch," I said, trying to bend my legs so the fabric would move away from my body.

"The way you wiggle, don't blame me if the dress doesn't fit," Sari Neni said. She gave the hem a yank.

"They never do anyway," I said, remembering the ugly mustard-colored dress of first grade.

Suddenly Apa filled the doorway with his tall frame.

"What are you doing here?" I stammered.

"You, Maria, are terribly spoiled. You will never talk like that to anyone again, ever. Do you understand? Do you think that because your mother cannot hear you, you can say whatever you please? This, Maria, is over. Now you will go to your room and write an apology to Sari Neni and to your mother."

Sari Neni unpinned the shoulders of the dress and it fell in a heap to the table. I stood shivering in my underwear. Then, crying, I slithered to my room.

My parents were yelling in the hallway. I heard talk of shoes and dresses and money, louder and louder. I covered my ears with my pillow, but the sound snuck under the fabric. Anya was crying again. I wanted to go out and tell her I was sorry. But why was I always sorry after the fact? Just like Apa, I was sorry too late. The door slammed and it was quiet.

I turned on my desk lamp and began to write. To Sari Neni and Anya I apologized for my behavior. Then I worked some more on my story about Little Lord Schnurmacher. He was on a ship, on his way to freedom in America. As the sun set outside my window, Little Lord Schnurmacher watched the sun rise behind the Statue of Liberty in New York. Unfortunately, he was terribly seasick and threw up right in the harbor. As I wrote, my stomach felt queasy. I put my pen down and glanced at the clock. Almost 10:00.

There was a knock on my door. "Marika, are you asleep?" Andras whispered.

"No."

He stood by my chair. "England and France declared war on Germany. Now it's official."

"What's official?"

"The war."

"Well, Apa's been talking about war for about as long as I can remember."

"I guess he was right," Andras said.

"He usually is," I said, remembering Sari Neni and the dress. "But I don't see what difference it makes to us whether the war is official or not." Uncle Lipot's stories about World War I seemed so long ago. Someday this war would be like that too. I yawned.

"Just thought you might be interested," Andras said, turning to leave.

The Chosen People

September 1939

Zsofi was waiting for me in front of the school building. "Mari, I've missed you," she said, hugging me with her bony arms.

It didn't take long to catch up on each other's news. We had read some of the same books, it turned out, only I had read them on the breezy porch at Vac and she had read them in the back of her father's tailor shop by the big hot irons.

"Mari, it was so hot in there, I thought I was going to die," Zsofi said.

My stomach flipped. I should have listened to my father and invited her to Vac. "Couldn't you find some other place to read?"

"Not when I was supposed to be watching the irons." Zsofi smiled. "Finally two weeks ago Papa decided that I wasn't contributing much to his business, so I got to stay home and read." Zsofi looked serious again. "The only problem is that my father might not be able to contribute much to the business either."

"What do you mean?"

"Papa says soon Jews aren't going to be allowed to run businesses."

"What are you going to do?" I asked.

"I don't know. Papa's been praying a lot and fighting with Mama. She says all that praying has gotten us nowhere for thousands of years, and it won't get us anywhere now. Really, though, I don't know what she thinks he should do."

I tried to imagine Zsofi's mother fighting. She seemed so calm, so sensible, so unlike Anya. "Well, I don't think they'll really close all the Jewish businesses," I said.

"That's what I say," Zsofi said, "because then what businesses will be left?"

Zsofi was right. The baker was a Jew, and so was the grocer. I thought about my father. Why hadn't he said anything to me about this rumor? Was he going to have to close his business, Schnurmacher Pal and Company?

A few girls came over and asked us how our summers were. They looked much more grown up than Zsofi and me. Two of them had new stylish haircuts. One of them said she had played a lot of tennis over the summer. I nodded. They drifted away from us, toward the boys on the other side of the fence.

"Hey, guess what I'm reading now," Zsofi asked.

We reached into our book bags, and at the same time we pulled out identical copies of *Oliver Twist*.

"I just knew it," Zsofi said. "What chapter are you on?"

"Eleven."

"I knew it again."

At recess we sat in the corner of the playground and read out loud. Poor Oliver. The conditions in Mr. Bumble's workhouse were deplorable. "How can people do things like that to each other?" Zsofi asked. "It's awful."

"And that Fagin. He's worse than Mrs. Voros," I said. Mrs. Voros was our gym teacher. She always put me and Zsofi last in line just because we were Jewish, even though short kids like us were supposed to be in front.

"Why do you think Dickens called Fagin 'the old Jew'?" Zsofi asked.

"Because he was Jewish, I guess," I said.

"I know that." Zsofi looked at me like I was stupid. "But he could have made him anything he wanted. He's the author, you know."

That was Zsofi, always thinking beyond what was written on the page. I just read to make sure poor Oliver was okay, but Zsofi read for more. "Well, some Jews are terrible, you know. Maybe he knew a Jew like that," I said, defending Dickens.

"I still don't think Dickens should have made Fagin Jewish," Zsofi said. "People will think the rest of us are like Fagin."

"Most people don't read *Oliver Twist*," I said.

"That's not the point," Zsofi insisted.

"Well, we can't make all Jews perfect, can we?"

The bell rang. Our fifth-grade teacher welcomed us back and wished us a good school year. She wrote our schedule on the blackboard. Our first class would be religion, followed by math, biology, and Hungarian history. A few minutes later the priest came in and wished us good morning and a good school year. Zsofi slipped out into the hall.

When I got home I asked Apa if I could stay out of religion class like Zsofi. "We're not really Catholic anyway," I said.

"It won't hurt you to learn a little about the Bible, you know," Apa said.

"I don't learn a thing in there. Anyway, I don't believe any of it."

"Marika, believing has nothing to do with it. We don't believe in Judaism either, right?"

I would not let it go. "The other kids know that I'm not a real Catholic. Anyway, I'd much rather stay with Zsofi and read. She'll get ahead in *Oliver Twist*, and then she'll have to wait for me to catch up."

"Maria, you can read at home. It is better for you to fit in with all the other children. Who knows, being Catholic may save your life."

The discussion was over. That was Apa's way, always

going along with the group and trying to predict what would "save our lives." Ever since I was born, he acted as if death were around the corner. *Learn French, it may save your life. Be Catholic, it may save your life.* I was tired of doing everything just because it might help me someday. What about right now? All Apa cared about was what things looked like on the surface, not what they really were. He was so proud that I was a pretty girl. What he meant was that I didn't look Jewish. Sometimes I wished J-E-W were written across my forehead. For Zsofi, with her red hair and long nose, there was no question about her ancestry. Zsofi could never pass. She never had to try to fit in. She could stay out in the hall during religion class and read whatever she wanted.

On Sunday during mass I heard some kids whispering from the bench behind mine. "She isn't Catholic. She shouldn't even be here." I tried to concentrate on the words of the priest. Here and there I understood a Latin phrase. Maybe someday I would be able to converse in Latin like the priests. The organist played a familiar tune. I had a terrible singing voice, but still I sang the words with my classmates and the church choir. Then I heard the whispering again, and the words got stuck in my throat.

From then on, I read through every mass. I put my book under my jacket on the way to church and sat in the back reading instead of listening to the priest. The only problem was that the church was freezing and my fingers turned blue and stiff. There was nothing I could do to warm them up. I tried breathing on them and rubbing them together, but they just turned a darker purple. The chapel was particularly cold, and when I got home Apa tried to warm my hands in his big hands. Uncle Lipot held them in his near the heater. Slowly the circulation returned and they got red and swollen.

"This child should be excused from mass," Uncle Lipot told my father. "One of these days she's going to get frostbite in that cold church."

Apa took off his glasses and put down the newspaper. "You really mean it?"

"Look at her fingers."

Apa held my puffy hands in his. "Okay, Mari," he said, sighing. "I'll write a note to the priest." Apa looked so upset that I wished I had never made such a fuss about the religion class.

Uncle Lipot tried to cheer my father up. "Why are you so gloomy?" he asked, forcing a smile. "And just today, when you got the necessary forms. Listen, all this will end sooner than you think."

My father shook his head.

"What forms are you talking about?" I asked.

Apa sighed and cleared his throat. He rubbed my hands for another minute and then stopped with my hands still warm inside his. "Now listen and don't tell this to anyone, not even Zsofi." Apa was whispering, even though there were only the three of us in the room. "I bought blank identification papers. They cost a lot of money, you cannot even imagine how much, and they were very hard to get. You will be the one to fill them out."

"What do you mean, identification papers?"

"Papers that say who your parents and grandparents are. Papers that prove we are Catholic. Papers that don't say *Jew* anywhere at all," Uncle Lipot said.

"But why am I the one to fill them out?"

"We all know about your handwriting talent," Uncle Lipot said.

"Everything on the forms will be exactly like the original identification papers except for the one line which says religion. There you will write *Catholic* instead of *Jew*," Apa said. He seemed to have trouble catching his breath as he spoke.

I spent the rest of the afternoon carefully filling in the papers. We left one form blank just in case it had to be filled in differently one day.

Apa wrote a note to the priest explaining the medical condition of my hands and asking that I be excused from mass. I gave it to him the following Sunday. "Maria, you are very good in Latin," he said. "It is a shame that you will no longer be attending mass."

I looked down. For a minute I thought that I might actually miss going to mass. I liked some of the songs and the Latin prayers.

The priest turned away. On the way home I felt like everyone else in the whole world was at mass except for me and Zsofi. I decided to stop at her house.

We went for a walk around the block. She told me about a romance she was reading. The man was in love with another man's wife. Then I told Zsofi about my father and Sari Neni.

"Tibor and Tamas's mother?"

"Yes."

Her eyes opened wide. "Hey, someday you three might be step brothers and sister," she said.

"No way. My father is still married to my mother. He can't get a divorce because Anya won't agree, and they had a Catholic wedding and everything."

Zsofi was thoughtful. "Your life is so exciting. My family is boring and ordinary, and to top it off, my parents won't stop fighting."

"I wish my family were more boring," I said.

"Think of the stories you'll have to tell your kids," Zsofi said.

"You're the lucky one," I said, remembering the warm milk and sweet rolls Zsofi had after school every day.

"Actually, neither of us is so lucky," Zsofi said. "My father said he wonders why Jews are called the chosen people when it seems we're always chosen for the wrong things."

"At least we were chosen to be in the same class and to sit near each other," I said.

"That's true," Zsofi said as she turned in at her apartment building.

TIBOR AND TAMAS

January 1940

The weather was sunny and clear, so Zsofi and I decided to take the long way home from school. We were talking about how glad we were to be done with elementary school. Our new teachers treated us like grownups instead of little babies.

"Plus we get to watch all the older kids," Zsofi said. Then she lowered her voice. "Do you know Bela? That friend of my brother's? Have you seen his eyes? He's got the most beautiful dark eyes and blond curly hair."

"That Bela? He already has a girlfriend," I said.

"So what?" said Zsofi. "I didn't say I was going to marry him. Just because he has a girlfriend right now does not mean he'll have her forever."

"I know, but still, the point is that he's got one now," I said.

Zsofi looked irritated. "Don't you ever read romances?"

"No," I said curtly.

"Anyway, I know there's somebody you have your eye on," she said.

I looked hard into Zsofi's bulging eyes. "Who?"

"Adam, of course."

How did she know? I'd never said a thing about Adam, but Zsofi was right. He was the only boy I knew who was quiet and sensitive.

We took a little detour just in case we might catch a glimpse of Bela near his house. All we saw was an older lady who she thought might be his grandmother, and a couple of small boys huddled inside their jackets. Zsofi was disappointed. "Maybe we could wait here on the corner for a few minutes and see if he comes," I suggested.

Zsofi shivered. "It's getting late," she said. Then she put her arm through mine and together we headed away from Bela's house. Zsofi was quiet as we walked.

"What's wrong?" I asked.

"You're lucky," she said. "You're pretty."

I blushed. People told me often that I was pretty, but I never really believed it. "It's not like any of the boys look at me," I said.

"Just wait," Zsofi said.

I looked over at Zsofi's red cheeks. She wasn't pretty like models in magazines, but I loved the way her eyes told stories as she talked. Nobody else I knew had eyes like hers. And her red hair was thick and wavy.

"You're lucky your hair is thick," I said, running my fingers through my completely straight bangs. But Zsofi wasn't listening.

"Have you heard about the Nuremberg Laws?" she asked. "They have all these rules about who's Jewish and who isn't. Papa says that anyone with three Jewish grand parents like you is considered Jewish."

"Who says?"

"The law."

"The law where?"

"In Germany, of course."

"So if you're considered Jewish, then what?"

"Then you can't go to college and you can't own a business. There are all kinds of things you can't do."

Now it all made sense. That was why Apa paid all that money for false identification papers. That was why I had to forge them. Why didn't Apa tell me about those laws?

I stopped walking and turned to Zsofi. "Germany is Germany and Hungary is Hungary. You're starting to sound like my father. Now come on." Then I thought that maybe the blank identification paper could be for Zsofi. The papers were expensive, but still. Maybe he could get more, for Zsofi's whole family.

"Hey, guess what," Zsofi said. "Look who's up ahead." I looked up and saw a head of curly blond hair in the distance. Zsofi sucked in her breath and gripped my arm tightly. "Let's get closer so I can show you his eyes."

It was almost dark when I stepped through the front gate of my duplex, and there was Tibor.

"You scared me," I said, stepping back. "What are you doing out here?" He wasn't wearing a coat and his hands were deep in his pockets. His sweater was big, and he looked small inside it. "What's wrong?"

He shrugged and started walking around the house toward the apricot tree. I followed.

"Remember climbing this old tree?" I asked. It looked small and bare without leaves in the near dark.

Tibor nodded. Then we heard the notes of the cello floating down from the upstairs window, beautiful and pure. We both stood still, barely breathing. It was the cello concerto by Dvorak, played from beginning to end without a single mistake. When the last note faded, I saw that Tibor had tears in his eyes.

"I'll never be as good as he is," he said. "No matter how much I practice and how much my father shouts at me."

"Yes you will," I said automatically.

"I won't," Tibor said loudly. "You don't know. Tamas is really talented. Me, I just practice a lot, that's all. My sound isn't pure like his."

I didn't say anything for a minute. Tibor was shivering. "We better go in. It's freezing out here," I said.

He shook his head.

I tried to change the subject. "How's school?"

"Okay."

Then we were quiet, both of us shivering. Tamas was playing a scale. He missed a note and started over. I tried once more to get Tibor to go inside, but he still refused. I didn't want to leave him out there alone under the apricot tree.

The door of the house opened and out came Apa, all dressed up in his best suit. Sari Neni was with him, also dressed elegantly in a long dress and black coat. They didn't see us. She was leaning on his arm and laughing. Apa opened the door of the car for Sari Neni. When she had pulled her long coat onto the seat, he shut the door gently and went around to the driver's side. Apa turned on the engine, and in a cloud of blue smoke they pulled out.

We heard the cello again, this time playing scales perfectly over and over. Tibor and I looked at each other.

"How long have you known?" Tibor asked me.

"A while."

"Why didn't you say anything to me about it?"

"You didn't say anything either," I said.

"It took me a while to be sure," Tibor said.

"Apa told me at Kekes."

"Were you surprised?"

"Totally. And what about your father?"

"There's not much he can do. He just goes to work with your father as always, and tries to pretend everything is normal."

Tibor was shivering uncontrollably. My throat was on fire and my hands were starting to hurt. The cello stopped. The window opened and Tamas stuck his head out. "You are going to get frostbite out there, and then you'll really not be able to play. Now get yourself in here," he said, and shut the window hard.

"Come on," I said, taking Tibor by the shoulder and leading him back to our house. In the stairwell, he paused for a minute.

"Thanks," he said.

"For what?"

"I don't know," he said. He seemed embarrassed.

"There's nothing to thank me for," I said.

In my bed I could hear Tibor practicing his scales and his father's loud voice interrupting over and over. For a long while I couldn't sleep. The sound of Sari Neni's laughter was still in my ears. Apa had chuckled too. They seemed so happy. My throat was swollen; I could hardly swallow. That meant ten long days in bed with Anya hovering over me. The good thing was that whenever I was sick, Uncle Lipot came to visit. I would ask Uncle Lipot about those Nuremberg Laws. I would also ask him to get more blank identification forms for Tibor and Tamas and Zsofi. I hugged Maxi. "Maxi, your favorite uncle will come tomorrow. Isn't that great?" But Maxi did not help me the way he used to.

ANDRAS

February 1940

When Apa came for his Wednesday night visit, Andras was gone. Anya had no idea where he was. "Maria, have you seen your brother?" Apa asked.

I shook my head. "He left after school," I said. Andras did that a lot. He would set his books on his desk, grab a big piece of bread, and head out. Sometimes I was asleep when he came home.

Apa went into Andras's room, and from the doorway I could see him looking through the books and papers on my brother's desk. Apa took one of the papers over to the lamp to see it better. It was a report card. Andras had failed both math and Hungarian history for the first semester of his twelfth-grade year.

Apa's face got all red. "Maria, did you get your report card today?" he asked, trying to control the shaking in his voice.

"Yes."

"May I see it, please?"

I had a perfect "1" in every subject except gym.

Apa patted my head. "Excellent, Marika." He put my report card next to Andras's on the table and shook his head. Then he paced back and forth in the living room.

The clock in the hall struck nine o'clock, and still Andras was not home. "Time for you to go to bed, Marika," Apa said. I got into my pajamas quickly and buried myself under my down quilt. When Apa came in to say good night, the lines around his eyes looked deeper than usual. Was he really that worried about Andras? I was sure my brother was just wandering around the city as usual.

"Good night, Apa," I said. "How long are you going to stay here?"

"Until your brother comes home," Apa said.

I woke up to lots of shouting. "What are you going to do with your life?" Apa yelled. "You are almost nineteen years old, and still you think you can read trash for a living?" I heard a thump in the garbage can that I knew must be Andras's stack of magazines. "Failing classes and reading trash will not get you anywhere!" yelled Apa.

"Neither will anything else," Andras answered calmly.

"If you continue to do nothing, you will be drafted into the labor camp. Do you know what that means? You will be a slave. You will dig ditches all day for nothing but a bowl of soup. Have you thought of that? I told you before, Jews are exempt from the labor camp only if they get into university, and if you fail history I cannot even get you into a small-town college." Apa was trying to control himself. "I am not saying get a one. Just pass. There are no more strings that I can pull for you. They have become threads. Please, Andras, try."

Andras didn't answer for a few minutes. Then he said quietly, "You know as well as I do that there is no future for a Jew. Not for me or you or Marika." Was Andras just finding an excuse not to study? Did he really think there was nothing that a Jew could do? I remembered my discussions with the actor at Kekes. I would be an explorer, a scientist, a writer. Did Andras really think that a man named Hitler in Germany would stop me?

"I told you about the false papers. You were baptized. You are not circumsized," Apa said to Andras.

"It's not going to make any difference," Andras said. "Everyone already knows that we are Jewish."

"All we can do is try," Apa said softly.

After Apa left, I got out of bed and tiptoed over to the garbage can. Quietly I took out all the magazines and returned them to my brother. He was on his bed reading *Hungarian History of the Middle Ages*.

"Thanks," he said.

"Remember when you saved Maxi from the garbage?" I asked.

Andras smiled. "Of course I do. I also remember how you hid under the piano, waiting for your chocolates."

"That was a long time ago," I said.

"But I remember the taste of those bonbons," Andras said.

"Do you still remember before the wall?" I asked.

"Of course. Don't you?"

"Barely," I said.

Our winter break was lengthened because of a coal shortage. That meant no Zsofi for weeks at a time. And no Adam. Zsofi had said she noticed him watching me when I walked out of the schoolyard. It was just a matter of time before he would offer to walk me home, she told me. I wasn't sure.

Andras and I huddled under the blankets at home. Andras tried to warm my hands in his, but no matter how much he rubbed them, they still had a purplish tinge. I held my book with my hands under the covers, but I kept dropping it. Andras made me a book stand out of wire so the only time I had to take my hands out was to turn the pages. At noon we listened to the BBC on Andras's short-wave radio. The newsman spoke first in Hungarian and then in German. In both languages the message was clear. London had been bombed. Most of France was under Nazi occupation. Nazi Germany was winning the war.

Every morning I listened to the radio to find out if the

schools were open. Finally, when the temperature stayed above freezing for three days, the announcer said we could return to our schools.

Zsofi hardly greeted me in the classroom. "What's wrong?" I asked.

"My brothers are gone," she whispered.

"Gone?"

"They were drafted into the Hungarian labor brigade."

"You mean they are being forced to fight for the Hungarian Nazis?"

"We heard..." Her voice cracked. "We heard that the Hungarians are using the Jews as a human shield. They are forced to march ahead of the troops. They dig the trenches for the troops, but they are not allowed to use those trenches." Zsofi took a deep breath.

The teacher was saying something about the human heart. All I could think of was a human shield. What exactly did Zsofi mean? I glanced over at her. She had the biology book open to the wrong page. I heard the teacher call my name and I stood up.

"Maria, tell us the name of the lower chambers of the heart."

My mind went blank. I had no idea. Who cared about the chambers? I felt dizzy for a minute. Human shield. Human heart. Zsofi formed a V with her fingers.

"Ventricles," I said, and sat down.

I started listening to the BBC on Andras's shortwave radio all the time. I even listened to the English broadcast to see if I could catch a few words. The name "Hitler" was the same in all languages. The German troops were advancing in Russia. Apa had a small world map and with red pins he marked the location of the German troops. Each day he moved them farther east. When I went to school, I told Zsofi every detail because her shortwave wasn't working. We tried to figure out exactly where her brothers were. I told Zsofi that they were probably hiding somewhere, waiting for the war to end so that they could come home. That seemed to comfort her a little.

Even though the weather was warmer, my hands were still purple. I glanced at Adam as I left the school building. I wished he could warm my hands in his. His fingers were long and graceful. He moved them as he spoke to his friend, but he never looked my way.

Zsofi didn't get any letters from her brothers. Each day she looked thinner and the circles around her eyes were dark. "They are just waiting until it's safe to come home," I told her as we walked away from the school building.

Zsofi looked up at the bright green leaves on the trees that lined the street. "It is already summer," she said softly.

Andras and I took the train to our summer house in Vac. When we got off the train, a warm wind was blowing from the west. I took a deep breath. "I love summer," I told Andras. I stopped to look at some wildflowers blooming by the side of the road.

We walked slowly toward the front gate of our house. Something looked different. All over the white fence were swastikas, the symbol of the Nazis. Across the top of the fence somebody had painted *Dirty Jews are not wanted.*

"We're not going in," Andras said.

"It was probably just those same boys who called me a dirty Jew," I said.

"You never told me about that. Anyway, we're not going in. We're taking the train back home."

"Right now? We can at least stay for a few days. I'm telling you, Andras, it was just a couple of kids."

"Even if it was, we're not staying here."

"Can we at least go to the river before we leave?" I took another deep breath of the warm air and Andras gave in. We took a drink at the well and then crossed the street to the riverbank. I found a round, flat rock and gave it to Andras.

"If it skips more than ten times, we'll survive the war," Andras said.

"You're starting to sound just like Apa," I said.

The rock bounced lightly on the surface of the water. It hovered for a minute and skipped eleven times.

"You did it," I said.

"There's one thing I've decided," said Andras. "If I

survive this war, I'm leaving this country forever."

"Where are you going to go?" I asked.

"Anywhere far away from here."

"America?"

"Maybe."

"Will you take me with you?"

"If you want to come."

"Maybe we can find Georg. Remember him?"

Andras nodded.

"He must be big by now," I said.

"If he survived the trip."

"What do you mean?"

"They were headed through Romania and across the Black Sea, and that is a very long way to flee from the Nazis."

We took the train back to Budapest and arrived in the evening. Everything seemed perfectly normal for a Saturday night. Lots of people were in the restaurants and cafés. Summer in Budapest would seem long. Zsofi would be helping in her father's shop. Tibor and Tamas had to practice their instruments for five to six hours a day. I had finished all the books I owned.

The next day was hot and humid. Andras asked me if I wanted to go to the swimming pool.

"I don't feel like it," I said. "I don't like to swim laps."

"We could go to the Palatinus pool on Margaret Island.

It has a shallow area, remember? You don't have to swim laps."

I hesitated. I didn't really like swimming ever since the time at Kekes that I almost drowned. But the Palatinus pool was nice. It was on an island in the middle of the Danube River, in a big grassy area. From there you could see the parliament building and business district on the Pest side of the city and the wealthy homes in the hills of Buda on the other. When I was little, I liked to watch the barges going up and down the river.

"Okay," I said, "let's go."

The water in the pool was freezing. A few people were swimming. One of them came closer. His hair was black and curly. Could it really be him? Adam got out of the pool in one graceful move and stood up, catching his breath.

"Hey, Marika, how are you?" he asked, coming closer. I introduced him to Andras and they shook hands. His manner was friendly and easygoing. We sat together on the edge of the pool the entire afternoon.

On the way home on the streetcar, Andras kept smiling at me. "Glad you decided to come along?" he asked.

After that, Adam and I met at the pool several times a week. We talked about our teachers and books we'd read. I wanted to ask him about his parents and his sister, but I didn't want him to think I was prying. I asked Anya if I could get a new swimsuit.

"Ask your father," she said. "He's the one with the money."

I didn't feel like asking Apa, so I just sucked in my stomach as best I could.

When school started again, I hoped Adam would be waiting for me by the gate, but when I saw him in the morning, he just waved and walked ahead with his friends. Zsofi said I should be more forward.

"Like how?" I asked.

"Ask him to walk you home."

"I can't do that," I said.

"Want me to do it for you?" she asked.

"No thanks."

OCCUPATION

February 1944

One sunny February day when I was in tenth grade, I saw Adam waiting by the gate after school. He must be waiting for someone else, I thought. But he said a friendly hello and walked between Zsofi and me.

"So, how've you been?" he asked.

My mouth felt dry and my tongue too thick to answer. "Fine. I'm fine," I mumbled.

Zsofi started to turn down a side street near the school. "Where are you going?" I asked her.

"I have to pick up some flour for my mother," she said, hurrying off.

Adam walked with me to the bottom of my street. He asked me all about my school schedule and my new teachers. He told me about his soccer game the day before, and how he had a bruise on his shin where his friend Laszlo had kicked him. He pulled up the leg of his pants so I could take a good look at the bruise. Just as he turned to head down the hill, our shoulders touched. "See you tomorrow," he said.

I wanted to run home and tell everyone I saw that Adam had walked me most of the way home and that our shoulders had touched. But tell who? I walked through the front door as if nothing special had happened. Anya was with the cook, discussing the lunch menu. I slipped into my room, sat down at my desk, and tried to write a poem, but the words sounded silly and forced. Instead I wrote *Adam* in all kinds of fancy calligraphy.

From then on, Adam waited for me every day, and every day Zsofi came up with another errand. Finally I grabbed her by the shoulder.

"Why won't you walk with us?" I asked her.

"He's your friend, not mine," she said.

"Come on, we can all be friends," I said. "Don't you like him?"

Zsofi was stubborn. Then her face lit up for a minute. "Hey, has he kissed you yet?" she asked me.

"I'm telling you, we're just friends. We've never even held hands."

Zsofi rolled her eyes. "Well, it wouldn't hurt if you took his hand first. He probably thinks you don't even like him. You know, he won't be patient forever."

How could Zsofi always be so sure?

Over spring break, Andras and I went to spend a couple of

days with Uncle Lipot and Aunt Ila at their summer house. Their cottage was secluded behind a small woods and close to a stream. Andras was reading a textbook in the seat next to me on the train. Ever since he'd been admitted to college in Debrecen, he barely paid attention to me.

I took out an art book I'd brought with me and opened it to my favorite picture, van Gogh's *Starry Night*. I loved the swirls of blue and yellow paint with the strokes so clear. "Don't you love this picture?" I asked Andras. He didn't answer. I stared out of the window and tried not to let him spoil my mood. We passed a few small farmhouses and fields that had just been plowed. I breathed on my hands and rubbed them together. Even though it was March, the weather was still cold. Soon I would warm my hands by Uncle Lipot's pot-bellied Franklin stove. We called it Frank as if it were a member of the family. Then Uncle Lipot would tell stories about World War I.

When the train pulled into the station, Uncle Lipot was waiting on the platform. His face lit up as soon as he saw us, and he opened his arms, ready for my big hug. The three of us took a shortcut through the woods to the cottage. Frank was burning brightly. I took a seat right next to the stove, and in a few minutes my hands were tingly and hot.

"Don't hold them so close, Marika," Uncle Lipot said. "Let them warm up slowly."

I sat back and sipped the hot cocoa that Aunt Ila had

prepared for us. Frank's glass belly was full of orange and blue flames. Andras seemed more cheerful.

"Tell us a story, Uncle Lipot," I said.

"How about you tell one today," Uncle Lipot said.

"I don't have any to tell," I said. "Nothing interesting has happened to me. I won't ever have good stories to tell my children like you do."

"Just wait," Uncle Lipot said. "You will have stories too. Only I hope they are not stories about war."

Instead of telling stories, Uncle Lipot and Andras discussed the latest developments in the war. "The partisans in Yugoslavia are fighting with each other," Uncle Lipot said, shaking his head.

"But Tito is winning," said Andras.

"Who is Tito?" I asked.

Nobody answered my question. The war, the war, the war. That was all anyone wanted to talk about. Except Adam. It was what I liked about him. He wasn't gloomy. He talked about soccer games and traveling and school.

"What are partisans?" I asked.

"Mari, we are trying to have a conversation," Andras said. "Can you please stop interrupting?"

I got my book and tried to read, but Uncle Lipot and Andras were talking so loud that it was hard to concentrate. I grabbed my jacket and opened the door.

"Where are you going?" asked Aunt Ila.

"Just out for a breath of fresh air," I answered.

It was so cold that I could see my breath. I pushed my hands deep into my pockets and looked up at the sky. There were so many stars here, far away from the lights of the city. Out of the corner of my eye I saw a bright blue streak. A falling star. When we were little, Andras told me that if you made a wish on a falling star, your wish was sure to come true. What would I wish? That Zsofi's brothers came home? That Georg and his parents were safe? I shivered in the cold night air and wished that Hitler was dead.

The next afternoon we headed back to Budapest. I wanted to stay another day, but Andras wanted to get back home. I hadn't even had a chance to talk to Uncle Lipot.

We got off at the train at the main station in Budapest, and there were lots of men in gray raincoats and hats.

"Who are they?" I whispered.

"Detectives."

"Detectives?"

Andras didn't answer. We waited to make our way through the crowded turnstile. Some of the graycoats pulled people aside and asked them for papers. They grabbed a man roughly by the collar and pushed him into a parked van. Andras took a folded piece of paper out of his wallet. He tapped the shoulder of one of the men and unfolded the paper.

"Officer, as you see here, I am a student at the College of Debrecen, home for the Easter holiday, and this is my little sister." Then Andras pushed the turnstile, and we were on the other side. He took my hand and pulled me quickly along the street away from the station.

"What was that paper?" I whispered.

"Shhh."

The wind was blowing through my thin tights. My legs were tired from trying to keep up with Andras. A van drove by. What if the driver pulled over and forced us inside? "Can we take a streetcar?" I asked.

"Be quiet and come on," Andras said, pulling even harder. The rain had started up and the wind whipped around us in gusts. I ran to keep up with my brother.

Anya was standing just inside the doorway of our house. Her face was completely white. She had no makeup on and her hair hung limply around her face. Grandfather was right behind her.

"You are safe, you are safe," he said, hugging us. "The Nazis have occupied Hungary."

YELLOW STARS

April 1944

The radio told us what to do. Jews were to report to a central office to pick up their yellow stars. We were to sew these stars onto our clothing and we were not to go out without the star clearly visible. I felt the blood drain from my face. How could we go around with big yellow stars like dunce caps sewed onto our clothing?

"What about the false papers?" I asked Andras.

"What about them?"

"They show that we are Catholic."

"Everyone around here knows us, Marika," Andras said.

Andras picked up our yellow stars at the local police station. I touched the stiff fabric. They looked like stars I made in first grade to decorate our Christmas tree except they had six points instead of five. Stars of David, Andras called them. To me they were clown stars, big and stiff and bright. If I met Adam, would he act as if he didn't see it?

Would he pretend? Maybe he had one on his sweater too.

I took out my sewing box with its spools of thread and needles stuck into a pin cushion. My hands were shaking so much I could hardly thread the needle.

"Do you want me to do it?" Andras asked.

I shook my head. "I can get it," I said.

Andras stood by my chair. "Just think of them as real stars," he said, "like in the van Gogh painting."

"Like the stars at the summer house," I whispered.

I thought about Zsofi struggling with the stitches. She had only three to sew because her brothers had already been taken. I stitched my own first, then Andras's and Anya's. The fabric was so stiff that my fingertips were raw from pushing the needle. With the tears in my eyes, I could hardly see where I was putting the needle.

I saved Apa's for last. People would laugh at him, Schnurmacher Pal, stockbroker, with a huge yellow star on the lapel of his jacket. I took my time placing it carefully so at least it would not be lopsided. Then I stitched around all six points.

A German car had parked right outside our house. Two officers got out and rang the bell to Tibor and Tamas's first-floor apartment. Andras cracked our front door so we could hear what they were saying through the stairwell. "I'm sorry to interrupt you," they said politely, "but this house has been selected as the German Officers' Club. You have twenty-four hours in which to vacate the premises. You may take what you can carry." Then we heard the clicking of heels, and they got back into their shiny black cars.

"That means us too," I whispered to Andras. His face was white. He held onto the door for a minute to steady himself.

"Mari, go to Apa's apartment and tell him what has happened."

I dropped Apa's jacket with the star onto the floor. The needle and thread were still attached. "Should I wear my star?" I asked.

"No. Just run. Very fast."

When I got up the hill I burst through the door of Apa's apartment. He and Sari Neni were sitting at the small kitchen table. I was so short of breath I couldn't even talk for a minute. Then the words came out.

"We have twenty-four hours to leave."

Sari Neni stood up and looked at my father with her eyes narrowed. "I told you so. I told you this would happen. Only you never listen to me," she said. Then she turned and walked slowly out of the kitchen.

Apa was controlled as always. "Mari, go home and pack up a few of your belongings in a small bag. Take only the most essential things. You and Andras, Tibor, Tamas, and their mother will come with me to stay with Mr. Danos. He has a villa outside of the city. Leo Bacsi will stay with a friend of his. Anya and your grandfather will go to your aunt Iren's on the other side of the Danube."

"What about the papers? Can't we show the officers our papers and tell them they have no right to take our house?"

"Mari, do as I say. The papers will be our last resort."

It was clear that Apa had planned this out long ago.

"Now walk home normally, as if nothing has happened."

"But I don't have the star."

"Just walk surely, calmly, down the hill. When you get home, do as I said. I will come and get you at six in the morning."

I tried to walk normally, but my knees were shaking so hard that I had to stop a few times. What if someone who knew me saw me without the star? All they had to do was tell a policeman and I would be shoved into a van like the man at the station. I tried to control my pace and the trembling in my legs. I counted my steps to keep from thinking.

When finally I got home, I told Andras and Anya the plan. I thought Anya might be hysterical, but she already had her bag packed, as if she knew all along that this would happen.

I looked around my room. The paper and ink were stacked neatly on my desk. My books were arranged on the shelf in order of height. *Anne and Julien* was the first, since it was the tallest. Next came *Little Lord Fauntleroy*. Maxi was lying on my bed.

I packed two sweaters, two blouses, two skirts, two pairs of socks. How long would we be gone? It was hard to cram everything into one small bag. I tried to put Maxi on the top, but his head was too big. Anyway, I was much too old to take an old rag doll. Apa said only essentials. At the last minute I picked up a poem Adam had given to me. Nothing romantic, just a few lines about sunshine and swimming pools.

That night none of us could sleep. Anya walked around the apartment, picking up small figurines and putting them back on the shelves. The light was on in Andras's room, so I went in. He was reading his magazines. We read a few of them out loud, taking parts. Then Andras warmed my hands.

We heard music coming from downstairs. It was Tamas playing the cello concerto by Dvorak. From beginning to end he played it through without anyone telling him to start over or play softer or louder. I opened the door a crack and Andras and I sat perfectly still, listening until the last note faded. Andras had tears in his eyes.

Mr. Danos was Jewish, so I wasn't sure how his house could be so safe, but maybe because it was out of the way the German officers would find it inconvenient. I wanted to ask Apa a million questions. How long would we stay? Would other people be there too? Sari Neni was trying to match her strides to Apa's. For a minute I wished she were

Anya. It wasn't working out between Apa and Anya, Andras had said. But nothing was really working out. I ran to keep up with Andras as we turned in at Mr. Danos's sidewalk.

Mr. Danos welcomed us warmly. His wife stood behind her husband, tight-lipped and stern. Then she took me aside and spoke to me like a six-year-old. "Marika, you are not to sit on the furniture. There are a lot of antique pieces, which will soil easily. You are also not to touch the dishes, which are, likewise, very delicate. We will find a special bowl and cup for you."

I wanted to ask Mrs. Danos where I should sit if the furniture was so delicate. Could I sit on the Persian rug or was that off-limits too? Maybe I had to read standing. When she wasn't looking I pulled a book off the shelf. The binding was leather. It was a copy of Homer's *Iliad*. When I tried to turn the pages, the tops were uncut; no one had ever read the book. I put it back carefully and chose another. Again, the pages had never been slit. It seemed that Mr. Danos collected beautifully bound books but never read them. I would have a lot to tell Zsofi.

Apa still went to work every day. Tibor, Tamas, and Andras played cards. Sari Neni rarely came downstairs. I sat in the library and read. Although Mrs. Danos had told me not to use the furniture, I found a chair that was more threadbare than the others, so I sat in it, and she didn't seem to mind. After a few days she became more friendly and even asked me about the books I was reading.

. . .

A week later, just after I had settled into my chair as usual, the doorbell rang. When Mrs. Danos opened it, I heard a man's voice asking to see Schnurmacher Maria. Surely he could not be looking for me. There must be a mistake. Where was Apa? Apa would hold me behind his back and ask the man to leave.

Mrs. Danos found me in the library. When I stood up, my legs buckled and I grabbed the arms of the chair to keep from falling. Mrs. Danos took me firmly by the arm and led me to the door. Two men stood in the entryway. They spoke in Hungarian, but they had swastikas on their sleeves and guns in their belts.

"Are you Schnurmacher Maria?" one asked.

"Yes, sir."

"But you are only a child. Where are your parents?"

"My father is at work. My parents are separated, so my mother does not live here." I tried to keep my voice steady.

"Come along with us now," they ordered, taking me by the wrist and pulling me toward their car. I looked back at Mrs. Danos. Her eyes met mine and for a minute I thought she might tell them to wait. Then the door shut and I was alone with the men. I still had the fancy book in my hands. Mrs. Danos would be angry that I took her book. The men shoved me into the car.

They didn't say anything to me or to each other. I looked out the window. We passed my old school and the

library. The driver turned up a broad street and stopped at
the rabbinical school. I'd been by there many times before
but never inside. Sometimes I'd seen rabbinical students
milling around the front door, but today there was no
one. The men opened the door for me and led me to the
registration desk in the front hallway.

"Are you Schnurmacher Maria?" a lady asked.

"Yes."

"Do you have a gold cigarette case?"

"No."

"A gold cigarette case labeled with your name was
found at the home of Mademoiselle Roullard."

"Mademoiselle Roullard was my French teacher, but I
do not have a gold cigarette case," I said. There was too
much saliva in my mouth. I swallowed hard.

"Go down to the end of the hall and turn right."

There in a small room were Anya and my grandfather.
Anya's eyes were glazed. She barely greeted me.

"What is this about a gold cigarette case?" I whispered.

"She is a very kind lady, Mademoiselle Roullard. She
promised me that she would return my cigarette case after
the war. It was a gift, you know, from your father. Real
gold. Eighteen carat," Anya said.

"What are you talking about?" I asked.

My grandfather pulled me close so that he could
whisper into my ear. "We had to turn anything valuable in
to the authorities. Rather than give up her gold cigarette

case, Anya asked Mademoiselle Roullard to keep it safe until the war is over. She must have labeled it with your name."

"The police came after me because of a cigarette case?"

My grandfather didn't answer.

Anya's face was sunken. My grandfather had his arm around her like a small child, and next to him she was really tiny.

We were led into a bigger room with forty or fifty people milling about. Nobody looked familiar to me. Some of them knew each other and stayed in small groups, whispering and looking around for more acquaintances. I caught a glimpse of red hair, and for a minute I thought maybe it was Zsofi. Then I saw that the face was broad and flat. I stopped looking around and stared at my own hands. I always noticed people's hands. My fingers were long and thin. Adam had long fingers with bony knuckles. I glanced around again. Lots of black hair but not him. I wasn't sure if Adam was Jewish or not. We'd been careful never to talk about the war, but now I wished we had.

My hands had turned blue. Grandfather tried to warm them up, but his hands were cold too. Soon an official came and told all the men to go down to the lower level. Anya and I were assigned to a small straw pallet on the first floor. Anya kept trying to smooth it out, but I told her to give up, straw was always lumpy. Then she smoothed out her skirt, over and over.

I sat on the pallet, but without my book there was absolutely nothing to do. I felt as if I hadn't slept in weeks, but when I lay down I couldn't sleep. Anya was right next to me. The faint smell of her perfume, mixed with the sweat of so many people, made me nauseated. I tried to scoot farther over, but then I was off the pallet. I gave up and lay there. Anya scooted closer to me for warmth. Why did Anya need a gold cigarette case? I had never known her to smoke. Why did Apa give it to her? I thought of the wall in my house, and Maxi, and all the books I'd left behind on my shelf. I stared at the ceiling covered with water stains and tried not to think.

Breakfast was tea without sugar. Lunch was watery soup and a piece of bread that was to last until the next day. Dinner was another bowl of soup. My stomach stopped growling after a few days and just stayed hollow. I wished I'd thought of bringing paper and a pen. I looked around the room at the other people. Some were lying down. Some were sitting and staring. Others were talking in groups. A few had books. I wondered if I could borrow one when they were finished. I remembered the book I had left in the police car. Mrs. Danos would be upset. She was always worried that her things would get damaged, and now I had lost a beautiful leatherbound volume. I shook my head to clear my thoughts. What difference would a book make now? Mr. and Mrs. Danos might be in another Jewish building along with Apa and Andras. Mrs. Danos with her brocade jacket and velvet dress might be sitting on a straw pallet like mine.

I had to do something. Latin verbs. I would start with first conjugation and recite all the forms in my head. Then I would move on to second. When school started again, Zsofi would be so impressed. *Video, videre, vidi, visus*. That reminded me of Caesar's famous words, *Veni, vidi, vici*: I came, I saw, I conquered. Just like Hitler, I thought, and I went on to third conjugation.

A girl came toward me. Her name was Agi, and she went to the school in the next district. She sat down on the edge of my pallet. "Do you know Varadi Istvan?" she asked me. I didn't. What difference did it make whether we knew the same people or not? "He's my boyfriend," she said. "Is that your grandmother?"

"My mother," I said, embarrassed. Agi meandered back to her own pallet. I went back to my Latin verbs.

Anya tried to talk to me too. For the first time she started telling me how much Apa hurt her when he left. "Sari stole Apa from us. She's a husband stealer and a whore," Anya said.

I looked around. Could anyone hear us? I tried to change the subject, but Anya persisted.

"Marika, did you hear what I said? She stole him from me. Worse than a thief." Anya's voice was getting louder.

"You don't have to yell," I said. "Do you want the whole room to hear that somebody stole your husband?"

Anya looked around. "Do you think they all know?" she asked, motioning to the ladies sitting on the next pallet. They eyed us suspiciously and Anya got quiet. Her hands were folded in her lap. She had chewed her finger-nails so short that her fingertips were raw. Her face was flushed. She started to say something else about my father.

"Stop," I whispered. "Tell me about your mother."

Anya's face softened. "I adored my mother," she said. "When I got scarlet fever, she nursed me back to health. She called every doctor in Budapest to cure me. Every single one." Anya put her mouth closer to my ear. "If it wasn't for my mother, I would have died."

I knew that Anya had had scarlet fever that left her mostly deaf, but I hadn't known that she had almost died. All the years that we'd lived in the same house, Anya had never talked to me beyond simple instructions about my dresses and shoes. Now she seemed to want to tell me everything that had happened to her over the past forty years, but she never asked me how I felt about anything or anyone, Apa, Andras, Sari Neni, Tibor and Tamas, Uncle Lipot. I wondered where they all were. Could they be in this same building, just downstairs with the men?

The door to the room opened and a few new people filed in. I looked for Zsofi, but there were no skinny red-headed girls with popping-out eyes. Anya was chewing her nails again. I looked away. So many people in the room, but I was all alone. There was too much saliva in my mouth all the time. My eyes were watery. I shut them hard and worked on my second-conjugation Latin verbs.

After breakfast, the fattest Hungarian guard asked for volunteers to be sent to a healthier place in the country-side. Everybody looked down at the floor. What would we do in the countryside? Maybe they would send us to those camps in Germany. The guard threatened to choose volunteers himself if nobody came forward. I tried to shrink. Anya crouched behind me. The guard walked up and down the rows. "You, how about you?" he said, pointing to Agi. She kept her eyes on the floor. "Answer me, will you."

"No thank you, sir," she whispered.

The guard moved on. The watery tea and bread came up into my throat. When finally he left, I went over to Agi and we sat together on her pallet.

"If you volunteer, they put you on a death train," Agi said.

"What do you mean?"

"A train that takes you to a death camp."

"How do you know?"

"I just heard it." Agi's voice broke and tears came to her eyes. I put my arm around her shoulders and we sat together for a long time.

Pea Soup

May 1944

Two weeks later, just after the guard had finished shouting his usual request, a scrawny boy ran up to me and shoved a brown paper bag into my hands. He ran away before I could ask him who he was or what he wanted. Inside the bag was a ham sandwich. I tore it in two, half for Anya and half for me. We gobbled it quickly, like animals, so nobody would know what we were doing. I imagined Mitzi Neni telling me to chew my food before I swallowed it. The scrawny boy brought us a sandwich every day, and every day we devoured it before anyone saw.

Despite the sandwiches, Anya's face became more and more hollow. I took her to the sink to wash up. First she wouldn't turn the water on. When I did it for her, she just stood there and rambled on about my father, her father, Sari Neni.

"Anya, wash your face," I said.

She stared at the water. "That's dirty water," she said.

"But it's water," I said. "Hurry up. There are other people waiting."

Anya splashed a little water onto her face. Then, with her face still dripping, she said how sorry she felt for Colette, that Colette was her only friend. After the war, she would go to Paris and find Colette. I remembered how Colette and Anya had discussed eyeshadow and rouge, but I never knew that Anya considered her a friend.

On our way back to our pallet, we heard an air raid siren and the thin, high whistle of a bomb coming closer and closer.

"To the basement," shouted the fat guard. The other guards hurried after him, and the last one locked us into our room before heading down himself. The bomb exploded, shaking our building like an earthquake. I covered my head with my hands, and in the dark I remembered throwing rocks into the river at Vac, some that skipped and some that sank, sending smaller and smaller ripples to the shore. I should have thrown a rock at the three boys, that's what I should have done.

The "all clear" sounded and the guards came back up. Agi walked over to me. "I like the bombs," she said. "They mean the Allies are getting closer and closer to victory."

"I know," I said, "but if we're killed by a bomb, does it make any difference who dropped it?"

"It does to me," she said.

. . .

After the air raid, the guard unlocked the door and came toward me and Anya. "Come with me," he said sternly.

"Me?" I asked, pointing to myself.

He nodded. My stomach dropped. What about the forged papers? Where were they? Wasn't this the time that I needed them?

"And my mother?"

He shook his head. "Only you. Hurry." Then he went and got three other girls and one boy, all about my age. One of them was Agi. He led the group of us past another guard, down the hallway to an office. A soldier sat at a desk stamping a stack of papers with an official-looking seal.

"Here you are," he said to the guard when he was finished. The guard took the papers and led us out into the bright sunshine. The streets were completely quiet. People were still in their basements because of the air raid. Only half of the building across the street was standing. Did the people in it make it to the basement? Did they have time? I looked away.

Soon we got to the office of a Jewish organization. The guard handed us the papers, motioned for us to go in, and then continued down the street and out of sight. All this could be a trap. We might walk into the arms of a Nazi officer. I remembered what happened to Georg's father with the Nazi officers who shot into the air as they pulled the rug. The sky was blue and the trees were just starting to bud. I could run away. I could find my way back to our house. Or Mr. Danos's house. But then what? The wind picked up. I shivered, then turned and opened the door of the office, the others behind me.

Inside the building a secretary told us to wait. Wait for what? A train to take us to the countryside? I remembered Georg playing with the small choo-choo train in my room. The secretary came back with four women who turned out to be the mothers of the other kids. They hugged their children, crying so that they could hardly speak. I sat there dumbly. Why did they bring me here? To watch mothers hugging their children?

The secretary asked if I was hungry, but I couldn't answer because my jaw was shaking. She disappeared into a back room and came back with a big bowl of split pea soup, which she placed in front of me on a small table. I bent my head close to the bowl and drank it as fast as I could. I thought only of the hot food in my mouth, sliding down my throat. Suddenly I heard a voice behind me. "I never knew you liked pea soup."

Apa's arms were around me so tight I could hardly breathe. Tears running down his cheeks soaked my shoulder.

In a low whisper Apa told me what had happened. He had found a high-ranking Nazi officer willing to take a bribe. Apa gave him 29,000 pengos, a small fortune, so that he could make an arrangement. The holding camp to which Anya and I had been taken was to be divided into two groups. One was for children up to age fourteen. One was for adults, ages sixteen and up. This left the fifteen-year-olds with no place to go; we were released into the custody of our parents.

"What about Anya?" I asked.

"There's nothing I can do," Apa said.

"She's all alone," I said.

Apa bent down so his eyes were level with mine. "Mari, please believe me," he said. "Please." His face was thin and pale. He was begging me. I looked away.

"What about Sari Neni?" I asked.

"She was taken along with Tibor and Tamas."

"Where are they?"

"I have no idea," Apa said, his voice breaking.

"What about Andras?"

"He was drafted ... He is a slave in a labor camp."

"Do you know where he is?"

"Not too far from the city," Apa said. "At least for now."

We walked to one of the specifically designated Jewish houses to which all Jews had been assigned. It was a high-rise near the Danube. On the outside was painted a big yellow star. We had a small flat to share with another family of four. The Nazi officers were still in our house, Apa said.

I tried to read a romance that the lady in the other family had finished, but I couldn't focus. What would Anya do at the rabbinical school all by herself? She would never go to the sink to wash up. She would wander aimlessly around the room, coming back to smooth her cut. The messenger boy Apa had bribed to deliver the sandwiches disappeared, so he had no way to send her the extra food. When I left the rabbinical school, I forgot to say good-bye to Anya. I also forgot to tell her never to volunteer for work in the countryside. I couldn't swallow. The tears on my face were warm and salty.

I sat by the window and looked down at the Danube below, flowing so peacefully along its banks. Lots of people wrote poems about the Danube. We had to memorize one in fifth grade about the wind blowing off the water. I recited it to myself, and when I was done, I sobbed.

ILONKA

July 1944

Apa went to work wearing his jacket with the yellow star. I wished he would stay in the apartment with me. What if he was forced into a van on the way? He came back to the apartment at noon for lunch, but all he would have was a cup of watery coffee and a piece of bread.

"You should eat," I said, "or you will get sick."

Apa took a bite of his bread.

After my weeks at the rabbinical school, I was starving. Apa watched me swallow a big spoonful of paprika potatoes and smiled a little. "You can eat my lunch," he said.

I wrote a few poems, but they seemed childish when I reread them the next day. I remembered *Little Lord Schnurmacher* and how hard I had worked on my manuscript that summer at Vac. All for nothing, it seemed now. Lots of things were all for nothing, the hours I spent practicing my handwriting, laughing with Zsofi, walking with Adam, dreaming of explorations at the South Pole. Zsofi was right: I should have taken his hand. But what did it matter now? Even the wall didn't matter since German officers had taken over our house.

In the evening when Apa came home, I opened the windows of the apartment, took a deep breath, and looked out across the Danube. Adam must be somewhere in this big city. Where was Andras? What about Tibor and Tamas? Where were they? Everything looked normal from so high up. Apa turned on the shortwave radio. I used to ignore the news, but now I put my ear close to the radio, trying to hear through all the static. The Germans had been beaten out of Paris and Rome. Budapest had to be next. The Russian troops were moving in. Already, in the evening when the city was quiet, we could hear the rumble of artillery coming from very far away. The Allies were fighting in the countryside east of Budapest.

There was a knock at the door. It was Artur, an old friend of Apa's. Apa greeted him gloomily.

"Pali," Artur said to my father, "you should be cheerful. The war is almost over. At least you have Marika here with you. That is more than most of us."

Apa sighed. "I know I should count my blessings. I also know that the Germans will lose this war. But it is not over yet."

Artur said quietly, "It can't be much longer."

"Maybe it cannot, but even a short time is too long. I made a large donation to the Mother Superior of the convent. She agreed to take Marika for the duration of the war, but then she changed her mind. I can't blame her, really. She said the Germans were suspicious of the convent. They already searched the premises twice for hidden Jews."

As usual I'd heard nothing about the convent plan. When I was little I'd thought of becoming a nun. I liked their flowing robes and big headdresses. There was something so solemn about the way they moved. But to think of going to a convent now ... Adam's curly hair and slender hands came into my mind.

"Your plan to get Mari out of the rabbinical school was perfect, Pali. Don't you think she is safe now?"

Apa shook his head. "They let her out, but that's all. They can come for all of us anytime, you know."

Artur came over to the cot where I was sitting and put his arm around my shoulders. "I'll tell you what, Pali. I have another plan for your Marika. You remember my fiancée, Ilonka? My dear Ilonka would be happy to keep Marika with her."

"Why doesn't she keep you?" I whispered, knowing that Artur was Jewish.

"Oh, Marika, if only she could. But that would be obvious. Everyone knows me there in her apartment building. But you? You could be her niece from the country-side. I'll go now and discuss it with Ilonka. I'll be back tomorrow night with more details."

Apa hugged Artur at the door. "Artur, think it over. This will put Ilonka's life in danger. You may change your mind. If you do, I understand."

The next day was longer than ever. I wrote a poem about the Danube but then tore it up. I wrote a few lines about throwing rocks at Nazi boys until their shins were bloody. When I reread it, the words didn't sound like mine.

In the late afternoon we heard a knock on the door. Artur was his usual cheerful self, but he talked softly so nobody else could hear. "Pali, Marika, it's all settled. Ilonka would like you to go over to her apartment tomorrow just so you'll know where it is. Then, when you decide the time has come, just go. Remember the address but don't write it down. Number 64 Julia Utca, apartment 4. Now I have to go." Artur hugged me and winked. "You'll see, my Ilonka is an angel."

"Wait, Artur, have you really thought this through?" Apa whispered. Artur waved his hand as if to say forget it. Then he was gone.

Apa told me to dress nicely, so I put on the checkered skirt and white blouse. Apa said we should wear our jackets with the yellow stars just in case we ran into somebody who knew us. I memorized the route to Ilonka's. Up the hill to the first streetcar stop. Change to the tram at Rakosi Utca. Walk past a cemetery and uphill again. When we got to the corner near Ilonka's apartment on Julia Utca, Apa told me to take off my jacket and fold it so that the yellow star was on the inside. He did the same with his jacket. We linked arms like any other father and daughter, and went to the third building, number 64, and up the stairs to the second floor. We knocked on apartment 4.

"Pali, Marika, come in. I've been waiting for you." Ilonka had set three coffee cups on her small table, and three sweet rolls. "Here, have a little snack, and we can discuss the particulars." Ilonka poured the coffee. "Now, Marika, you may never even need to use this plan, but if and when your father decides that the time has come, you will become my niece. Your first name is Maria, same as always, but your last name is Kis, and you have come from Szendro. That area has already been occupied by the Russians and you got separated from your parents. With no other relatives in Szendro, you found your way to Budapest to stay with me, your only aunt, the sister of your mother. So here you are."

I nodded.

"Can you remember all that?"

"I think so. I am your niece from Szendro. I got separated from my parents."

"That's right. Now both of you, drink your coffee and eat the rolls."

"How can I ever thank you?" Apa asked.

"Nothing to thank. I am doing what any normal human being would do. I only wish I knew someone who could do the same for Artur."

"I wish I could help," Apa said, drinking the coffee but leaving the roll.

"Now go home before it gets too late. The streets are dangerous. Just remember, whenever you decide the time is right, I will be waiting." Apa tried to thank Ilonka again, but she interrupted him. "Enough, Pali, enough. Now go."

The whole way home I kept repeating the story in my head. I couldn't hesitate if someone asked me who I was.

"Apa, have you ever been to Szendro?" I asked.

"Yes."

"What is it like there?"

"It is very small, with only one main street. On that street is one store and a post office. The streets are mud and gravel. There is no electricity. There are a few geese and chickens walking in the street."

"And where is my house?"

"It is behind the post office on the left."

I looked at Apa. He was concentrating hard on the details. I memorized them as he spoke. When we got back to the apartment, Apa took his wallet out of his pocket, and from it a folded piece of stained paper.

"Do you remember this?" Apa asked.

It was the one blank identity paper from so many years ago.

"Now is the time," Apa said. I sat down at a rickety desk with a small bottle of ink and an old-fashioned pen. I took a deep breath. It had been a long time since I had practiced my calligraphy. Carefully on the line where it said *Name*, I wrote *Kis Maria*. Where it said *Religion*, I wrote *Katolikus*. When I was done, Apa blew on the ink to make sure it was completely dry.

"I miss Uncle Lipot," I said softly to Apa.

"I hope he and Ila are okay," Apa said.

For the rest of the summer I stayed in the high-rise by the Danube all the time. My stomach felt queasy and unsettled. Why hadn't I told Anya never to volunteer for work in the countryside? Who knew where they would take her? Apa tried to find another messenger for the sandwiches, but there was nobody left to bribe. Anyway, he'd spent most of his money on my rescue from the rabbinical school. I played solitaire for hours. Apa played in the evenings. Whenever the game worked out, he would smile just a little and say, "The Allies are winning."

It was true, according to the BBC. The Allies were advancing fast. Still, Apa was gloomier than ever.

In September, for my sixteenth birthday, Apa got hold of a stack of books. I started the first one, *Pride and Prejudice*, right away. I knew I should try to make the books last, but once I'd begun, I read all day and the next. By the end of the week I had started the last one, *The Prince and the Pauper*. Tom and Edward seemed to be able to change identities easily enough. When the time came, I hoped I could do the same.

That night when Apa turned on the shortwave radio, there was so much static we could hardly hear. He fiddled with the controls, trying to get a clearer message, but then we couldn't hear anything at all. He turned on the regular Hungarian radio. There was a military band playing joyfully. Then an announcer came on. "This is Radio Budapest," he said. "A new government has been formed." All the blood drained from Apa's already pale face. "The Hungarian Nazi Party has taken over the government," continued the announcer.

Apa held on to the table to steady himself. "This is it." Then he took a deep breath and cleared his throat. "Marika, now is the time. You will go to Ilonka's. I will hide in my office."

"Right now?"

Apa bent down so he could kiss the top of my head. "Right now, Marika," he whispered into my hair.

We went down to the basement of our building where the janitor was waiting for us. Apa used the last of his money to bribe him to lead us through a series of passages connecting several apartment buildings so nobody would notice us leave. When we got outside, Apa squeezed my hand. That was all. I was on my own.

I didn't even have to think to remember the way. The sun had gone down, but the route was still clear. The streetcar, the tram, uphill to Julia Utca. What if Ilonka wasn't home? I turned the corner. There was the building, the narrow sidewalk, the two flights of stairs. I knocked. No answer. I knocked again. What if she didn't live there anymore? Where would I go? What if someone came and asked me what I was doing there?

I sat in the hallway rehearsing my story. Why hadn't I asked Ilonka more questions? Did her niece have any siblings? What kind of work did her parents do? The story had more holes than anything else. What should I say if one of the other tenants walked by? Should I say good evening, or nothing at all? What if Ilonka decided that hiding a Jew was too big a risk? Maybe she was inside but would not answer the door. I heard the door downstairs open and shut. I decided to say good evening to whoever came up before they had a chance to ask me anything.

There was Ilonka, her arms full of packages. "Marika, I got some bread to have with our evening tea," she said. I smiled weakly, forgetting to even try to help with a few of her parcels. "I had a feeling today would be the day," she whispered.

Ilonka had a corner all prepared for me. In it were a narrow cot, a lamp, and a few books stacked under the cot. We drank our tea quickly before it could cool off, and spoke little.

"Marika, go to sleep," Ilonka said. "Tomorrow is another day."

"Thank you," I said. "For everything."

Ilonka waved her hand at me. "No more of that. The toothpaste is in the cabinet by the sink. There is a cup for you on the left. Good night."

I was exhausted, but it took me a long time to fall asleep. I thought of more and more questions about Szendro.

In the morning Ilonka told me to stay as quiet as possible in the apartment while she was out. "If anyone asks me about you, I will tell them that you are my niece, but it is better if they don't ask."

I nodded. Apa had told me the same thing. "Do you know about the identity paper?" I whispered.

"Yes, I know." Ilonka squeezed my arm. "I'll stop by the office and make sure your father is okay." Quickly she fixed two sandwiches to take to him. Before she left, Ilonka picked up a small picture on her desk of Artur and her on the banks of the Danube.

"Do you know where he is?" I asked.

Ilonka shook her head. "I have no idea," she said, and her voice broke.

While Ilonka was gone I stayed on my cot except to go to the bathroom. I read through the small stack of books. The first one was a book of sayings and proverbs, most of which sounded good unless you thought too hard about them. I could just imagine Zsofi saying them in her mocking voice: *Don't put off for tomorrow what could be done today.* But what could be done today? Nothing. That was the problem; there was absolutely nothing to do, but if I did the wrong thing, I might not survive.

I immersed myself in a romance, but it was quick to read, and no matter how I tried to slow myself down, I could not stretch it out. I looked at my reflection in the small hand mirror I had brought in my bag and thought about Adam. My hair really was too straight. Too bad I didn't inherit a few of Uncle Lipot's curls. And my eyes were too deep. Zsofi always said that made me look mysterious, but that wasn't the look I was after. I wanted to look adventurous and capable, not mysterious. I pulled my hair straight back, but that only made my forehead look too big. I shook my head and let my hair fall onto my shoulders. How stupid to be thinking of hair styles and eyes right now.

That night there was an air raid. Ilonka and I headed down to the basement along with the other residents in the building. Ilonka introduced me to the lady from next door.

"This is my niece from Szendro," she said.

The lady shook my hand and looked me over. Did she wonder why she never heard about this niece before? Did she notice my black hair and think I was a Jew?

"Nice to have a visitor in these hard times," she said to Ilonka.

"Indeed," said Ilonka, patting my arm.

A week later, while I was eating a mostly shriveled apple on the cot, the doorbell rang. I sat up quickly and ran my fingers through my tangled hair. It rang again. Through the milky glass of the door I could make out the shapes of two people in black uniforms. It was too late to hide.

"Coming. Just a second," I said, using the time to collect my thoughts and slip on my house shoes. I opened the door. The two officers saluted me.

"Are your parents home?" they asked.

"No, sir. They do not live here. I am staying with my aunt," I answered.

"Where is your aunt?"

"She went to see if she could buy something to eat."

"Why are you living with your aunt and not your parents?"

At that moment I choked on the piece of apple still in my mouth and coughed for a few minutes, taking that time to rehearse my story.

"I am from Szendro. When the Russians came I lost my parents. I searched and searched for them, but they were gone. Finally I found my way to my aunt in Budapest." The story came to me easily. I felt tears come to my eyes as I spoke. I really was separated from my parents. The men saw me crying and stopped questioning. The shorter one looked hard into my eyes.

"May we see your papers?" he asked.

"Of course." I took my forged identity paper out of my bag and handed it to him. He looked at it for several minutes before giving it to his partner. This was it. The taller one would see that the ink was fresh. He held the paper up to the light. They would grab me, throw me down the stairs to their waiting car. The chewed-up apple came up my throat into my mouth. I wanted to snatch the paper and tear it up. A lie. That was what it was, a lie. I watched the officer's eyes as they moved over the words on the page. He looked up, thanked me, and handed back the paper.

"Do you mind if we look around?" the short one asked. "We hear that there are Jews hiding in this building. Do you know anything about that, young lady?"

"No, sir, but feel free to look around."

They took a flashlight and looked under the beds, in the closet, in the pantry. The short one asked if the sofa opened up.

"Yes, sir," I said.

They took off the cushions and pulled the sofa out into a bed. Finally satisfied, they returned to the front door.

"Thank you, miss," said the tall one.

"I hope you find your parents," the shorter one added.

They clicked their heels and went to the next apartment. I shut the door gently. Then I walked calmly into the bathroom and threw up. Even when my stomach was completely empty, I heaved into the toilet. Slowly I staggered over to the sofa and lay down. The room was spinning in circles when I shut my eyes. When I opened them, it was worse. I heard the officers leaving the building and my heart was pounding so hard that I could barely breathe.

The door downstairs clicked. I opened my eyes in the dark. The officers were coming back. The door of the apartment opened.

"Marika?" Ilonka came over and sat on the sofa. "What happened?"

"They came. Two officers, looking for hidden Jews."

Ilonka put her hand to her mouth.

"I told them our story and they asked for my identity paper. They looked at it for so long." My voice broke and I could not stop crying.

"Perfect, Marika, perfect. You did exactly the right thing," she said, patting my head. "Now we have to be quiet, Marika."

When I calmed down, I asked about my father.

"He wasn't there." Ilonka took a deep breath. "I'm sure he found a better place to hide. The office had no bathroom. Waste had to be dumped into the alley, which might become noticeable. Knowing your father, he found something better." Ilonka looked down. "But about Artur, I don't know." She swallowed hard.

"Maybe he found a better place too," I whispered. Better place. What would be a better place?

That night there was an air raid and we went to the basement. A neighbor said that he had seen four Jews hanging from the lamppost in front of the stock exchange that day. I was sure that Apa was one of them. Again I felt nauseated. What would I do after the war without Apa? Without Andras? I concentrated on sweeping out our corner of the basement.

Niece from Szendro

December 1944

The winter crept on. All the windows in the apartment had been broken by the explosions of nearby bombs. I spent most of the day huddled under a blanket. Ilonka stayed home too, but we talked little. Neither of us had the energy. We dozed and stared out the window at the frozen sky. I recited Latin verb conjugations inside my head until I was sure that if I went back to school I would be the star of the class.

I wondered if our house was still standing. Lots of buildings had been bombed. Somehow I thought that even if my house was hit, that wall would still be there. All by itself, just a wall in the middle of the rubble, with Maxi perched on top.

The day after Christmas, all the people in the building moved down into the basement for good. The cannon fire was so close that we were afraid a cannonball would hit the apartment. We used a small stove that sat in the corner to make tea and watery soup with whatever food Ilonka still had. Earlier she had bought a bag of flour that turned out to be rancid. We mixed it with water anyway and dried it into hard circles that smelled like mildew. I held my breath and swallowed as quickly as I could.

Getting water became a problem. The pipes in our apartment building were not deep enough and so the water in them had frozen. Ilonka sent me to get water from the building next door, which had a slightly deeper basement than ours. A few people waited ahead of me at the water spigot.

"I am so happy. The Jewish problem is now permanently over," one lady said.

The woman behind her nodded. "They are gone forever," she said.

"Eventually the Germans will win. They have some new weapon, have you heard?"

"I heard," she said.

It was my turn at the spigot. Water barely dripped out. One of the women looked at me.

"Turn the knob all the way around," she said, helpfully.

I tried to smile, but my teeth were chattering uncontrollably and my hand shook so hard that I dropped my bucket. What if she knew I was Jewish? She would tell a soldier and he would shoot at me.

I finally got the bucket filled and headed carefully back

toward our basement. Bullets whizzed over my head. The Russians and the Germans were fighting over Budapest, street by street. I stayed close to the building wall as I made my way back to the basement. Ilonka thanked me for getting the water. I didn't tell her about the ladies.

A few of the other people in the building tried to talk to us. They asked Ilonka about me, and she told them how I'd gotten separated from my mother, her sister, and how I hoped to be reunited with my parents after the war. One lady had lived in Szendro as a child.

"Do you remember the house behind the post office?" she asked. "That was my house."

"I remember," I said.

She stared hard at me. "Funny, I don't remember you at all," she said.

"Oh, Marika would have been a baby when you lived there. Of course you don't remember her," Ilonka said.

The lady kept looking at me. Did she know we were lying? I grabbed the broom and swept our basement corner.

Russian loudspeakers urged the people of Budapest to surrender and reassured the citizens that they would come to no harm. The sound of cannon fire changed to the sound of rifle fire. Ilonka said the Russians had advanced into the outskirts of Budapest. She thought the end of the war was near, but for me it was hard to believe. I imagined emerging into the winter air, alive and free. But free to do what?

"Marika, listen to me. I think the Russian troops will make it to our side of the street by tonight, but there is another worry. Russian soldiers are going door to door at night, looking for girls to rape. The best thing we can do is make you look too young." Ilonka began fixing my hair into two braids and tore an old blouse into strips to use as ribbons. She borrowed a doll from a family in another corner of the basement and told me to hug it all night long. Ilonka stood back to look at me. She nodded, satisfied. Then she put her hair up in a messy bun in back and untucked her blouse. "I will make myself too old," she whispered.

At night I heard voices at the door. Someone kicked the door open and the voices got suddenly louder. They shouted in Russian. Two of them had machine guns pointed in our direction. I closed my eyes. A flashlight beam roamed the room and landed on my face. One of the Russians spoke and I felt their steps come closer. I breathed slowly, in and out, in and out. The man said something else. The beam of light moved on and the door shut.

Ilonka came to my side. "We were lucky," she whispered. The officers would go to another building and keep looking. They would find another girl, one without braids and a doll. Ilonka held my shoulders and I sobbed silently in the dark.

The tiny basement windows were covered by sandbags, but I could still see through the cracks between them. Occasionally boots went past. There was the sound of bullets. I swept our corner for the tenth time that day. All the weeks at Ilonka's I hadn't felt this restless. Each minute seemed an hour. I glanced at my watch. Fifteen minutes had passed. The floor was cleaner than in the best restaurant in town.

There was absolutely nothing to do but try and stay warm. We stamped our feet, paced back and forth, huddled under blankets. I lost track of the days. Slowly, the streets became quieter. The fighting had moved on. Nobody in our basement talked; Ilonka and I said little. One morning three Russian soldiers came in with a big canteen full of soup. They handed me a loaf of bread and said something to me. I couldn't understand their words, but I thanked them and offered bread to the other people in the basement.

I stared at the windows and dreamed of going out. I could look for Apa, Andras, Zsofi. "Maybe we could go out and look for my father," I told Ilonka.

"Be patient, Marika," she said. "I made a promise to your father to keep you until he returns, and I plan to do just that."

I heard the front door of the building open. I looked at Ilonka. "Is Varadi Ilonka here?" someone asked. I thought it was Artur, but the voice was older and quieter. The sound of footsteps headed toward the basement. I jumped up from my mat on the floor and started running to the stairs, but I hadn't run in so long that my legs gave out and I fell onto the floor.

"Marika, I never knew you to be so clumsy," Apa said, bending down to pick me up. I held on to his bony shoulders and stood unsteadily on my own two legs.

"Apa," I sobbed. "Apa. Apa. It wasn't you."

"Who wasn't me?"

"The man hanging in front of the stock exchange."

Apa held me on his lap like a baby. When I finally stopped crying, I asked about Andras.

"He escaped from the labor camp, and we were hiding in the basement of Uncle Lipot's apartment building. It was safer there because my office was hit by artillery fire." Apa looked at Ilonka. "Artur will be back soon. It takes a while for people to get where they are going. The trains are not running."

Ilonka nodded. "Is it safe to go out?" she asked.

"The war is not officially over, but it seems to be safe enough right here," Apa said.

Slowly we went up the stairs to the front hallway and then out into the cold January air. Light snow had fallen and the sun was so bright I could hardly see. In the street, a Russian soldier waved to us. I tried to wave back, but my arms were like lead. In the front yard of the building, a frozen horse was lying on its side. A few people tried to get pieces of it with a hammer. I looked away, nauseated. Ilonka invited us into her apartment, where I gathered my few belongings.

Apa thanked Ilonka. "Someday if I have money again, Ilonka, I will pay you for this," he said.

"Don't even try, Pali, don't even try. Just bring my Artur home to me."

"That's the one thing I can't promise," Apa said.

"I know," Ilonka said, looking away. She took a deep breath. "Now go before the sun sets. Marika, come visit. I'll miss my niece from Szendro."

DANDELIONS

January 1945

Apa, Andras, and I stayed in the gym of the old Jewish high school along with other Jews who, like us, had no place to go.

"Why can't we go back to our house on Roka Utca?" I asked. It seemed so long ago that I'd been there.

"The bridges over the Danube have all been destroyed," Apa said.

"But the Danube is frozen."

"It may seem frozen, and I know some people have walked across it, but we have not survived a war only to drown in an icy river."

The city was in shambles. Bombed-out buildings leaned precariously on each other. Food was meager. Apa found an old friend who agreed to let us stay in his apartment. Apa, Andras, and I huddled together most of the day, me in the middle, trying to keep my teeth from chattering and my hands from turning completely blue.

Finally the weather warmed up a bit and the ground thawed. Huge bedbugs scurried around our mattresses all night. We spent as much time as possible outside, wandering around the streets, hoping to run into old friends. I walked by Zsofi's building, but only the back wall was still there. I scanned the streets for the black curly hair of Adam. I knew where he lived and considered going to his house, but what would I say to his mother? She didn't even know me. I walked down his street with Andras, but it was deserted.

Someone came to the apartment with a note from Anya. She wrote that she was in an American hospital in Germany, waiting to take a train home. I held the slip of paper up to the light from the window. The handwriting was shaky, but it was definitely Anya's. Andras and I went to the train station to wait for the four o'clock train. Anya was not on it.

"Maybe tomorrow," said a familiar voice. Not three feet away from where we were standing was Zsofi with her mother.

After that Zsofi and I met at the station each day. She was waiting for her father and brothers; I was waiting for Anya, Grandfather, Tibor and Tamas. Each day after the last train left, we walked all over the city, talking about the past year. Zsofi and her mother had spent most of the winter in the basement of their shop, huddled under unclaimed men's suits, after her father had been taken away.

"You should have seen me. I had on three suit jackets

and four pairs of pants all tied around my waist with string," Zsofi said.

I imagined skinny Zsofi with all those clothes on, and suddenly I couldn't stop laughing.

"Look," Zsofi said, pointing to a speck of yellow in the middle of a pile of rotten boards. "A dandelion."

We bent down to get a closer look. There were dandelions all over. I kicked a board. Underneath it were more buds. How could flowers have sprouted in a pile of rotten wood? I looked at Zsofi. In the sun, her red hair was brilliant. I picked a dandelion that had gone to seed and blew on it. A seed landed in her hair. I pulled it to the end of the strand and watched it float away.

A temporary bridge across the Danube was finally finished, so Andras and I went to take a look at our house on Roka Utca. On the Buda side of our city, things were worse than on the Pest side. As we walked uphill away from the Danube, it seemed that hardly a single building was left intact. It was hard to figure out exactly where we were with all the familiar landmarks gone. Andras pointed across the street and said, "Look, there's our elementary school."

"Where?"

"See that pile of bricks right there?"

My legs felt weak. "Let's rest a minute," I said.

"Don't you want to go see if our house is still standing?" Andras asked.

"I have to rest," I said, sitting on a crumbling curb. I wasn't sure I really wanted to find our old house. What if it too was just a pile of bricks?

But it was still standing after all, or half of it. The front gate was still there. Andras and I walked hesitantly up to the front door and knocked. Nobody answered, so Andras pushed open the heavy door. Straight ahead was Tamas and Tibor's first-floor apartment. To our right, the stairwell was dark but the stairs looked solid enough. We walked up slowly, placing our feet carefully between pieces of broken glass. The front room was okay, aside from glass and stones. I turned toward my room. The balcony was hanging by a single metal rod. All the furniture was gone except for my mattress. Across the hallway, the wall between Apa's apartment and ours was still standing.

"That figures," said Andras. "Remember how sad you were when Apa built it?"

I nodded. "Weren't you?"

"Not really. I knew all along what was going on."

"Why didn't you tell me?"

"You were just a baby."

"I wonder what happened to the rest of our stuff," I said, pointing to the empty walls where pictures once hung.

"Burned for firewood," Andras said. Suddenly he seemed in a hurry to leave. "Let's go."

"Wait. I want to look around."

"There's nothing much more to see in here anyway," Andras said.

We heard some footsteps in the hallway, and then a knock. There stood the lady who used to be the maid for our duplex. "Marika, Andras," she cried, hugging first me and then my brother. There were tears in her eyes. "I so much hoped it was you. Now wait. I have something for each of you, just a minute." She disappeared down the stairs and came back with two dirty paper bags. "This one for you," she said to me, "and this one for Andras."

Andras looked in his first. There was the old car made out of his Erector set. I opened my bag slowly, and Maxi looked up at me. I took him out. Except for a few new leaks, he hadn't changed a bit.

When we got back to the apartment, Apa said he'd heard rumors that a lot of Jews would be returning that afternoon, so Andras, Apa, and I hurried to the train station. Apa stood back, scanning the crowd. We heard the rumble of the train coming from far away. People moved restlessly. The light in front of the train grew bigger and bigger. The train screeched to a halt at the station.

After the doors opened, for a minute there was no one. Then slowly the people came off, weak and tired. The crowd made way for relatives as they rushed forward to meet their mothers, fathers, sisters, brothers. Some passengers had nobody waiting and just stood dazed in the late afternoon sun.

Apa's face turned pale. There, leaving the last car, were Anya and Sari Neni, side by side, leaning on each other. Wife stealer. Whore. That was what Anya had called her. An opera singer, laughing with my father, sitting with him at their kitchen table, their table in their own apartment. Now Sari Neni had her arm around Anya's hunched back. Sari Neni was helping my mother find her way. Tibor was slightly ahead of them. But where was Tamas? Where was his blond hair? The notes of his cello? Tibor's eyes caught mine. He smiled for a second.

The three of them made their way toward us. When they came close, I took Tibor's arm, Andras took Anya's, and Apa took Sari Neni's. The six of us walked silently away from the station.

Epilogue

Anya had been taken to the concentration camp at Auschwitz. Nobody knows how she survived, and when she came back, she was malnourished and more confused than ever. She lived with Andras in Hungary for several years before joining Marika in America.

Andras became a doctor and lived the rest of his life with his wife and son in Hungary.

Grandfather never returned from the concentration camp.

Uncle Lipot and Aunt Ila survived the war and lived out their lives in Budapest.

Tamas died in Auschwitz when an officer hit him with a rifle.

Adam never returned from the concentration camp.

Artur returned, and he and Ilonka got married.

Zsofi and her husband immigrated to America in 1956.

Zsofi's brothers and father never returned.

Leo Bacsi, Tibor and Tamas's father, survived the war.

He and Apa continued to be business partners for a short while until the stock exchange was closed by the communists.

Nobody knows what happened to Georg and his parents.

Sari Neni and Apa lived out their lives in Hungary. Apa got a job as an accountant. He visited Marika several times in America.

Tibor and his wife and twin daughters lived next door to Sari Neni and Apa. He and his family took care of Apa and Sari Neni in their old age.

Marika left Hungary in 1949 with her fiancé. They got married in Switzerland. From there they went to Australia and eventually to America, where they raised their family.

Andrea Cheng teaches English as a Second Language in Cincinnati, Ohio, where she lives with her husband and their three children. She is the daughter of Hungarian immigrants. *Marika* is loosely based on her mother's story.